MW01593534

Paradise Stories

Dustin Heron

small desk press • san francisco

Copyright © Dustin Heron 2007.
Cover Art © Joshua Evans 2007.

Book Design by Jacob I. Evans.

All rights reserved. No part of this book may be reproduced in any form or by any electronic or mechanical means including information storage and retrieval systems, except in the case of brief quotations for the purpose of reviews or critical articles, without permission in writing from Small Desk Press.

The characters and events portrayed in this book are fictitious. Any similarity to real persons, living or dead, is purely coincidental and not intended by the author.

Published by Small Desk Press
PO Box 170232, San Francisco, California 94117-0232
www.smalldeskpress.com

ISBN

978-0-9789858-0-6

Printed in Canada

For my family

"Paradise is not a story. It's about what happens when the stories are over."

—Charles Baxter

Table of Contents

Two Very Long Arms

When he was ten, a shit-field sprang up in Billy's front yard. It started in the house, coming back up and out the toilet. Water splashed out so fast the toilet lid flapped up and down in the rush. The dingy brown water spilled across the linoleum, old floaters and forgotten wads of toilet paper swimming towards the shag carpet, which became thick and wet with humid toilet stink; the whole house took on the atmosphere of a marsh.

Everyone was out of the house when it happened, and one by one they came home to clouds of stale piss and flies. When Billy's mom, Ant, came home from shopping, she saw the water running out from under the front door and went to her parents' house on the other side of town. When Billy got home, he opened the door and went slowly inside, squishing across the carpet for the phone. He called his grandparents and Ant came home. They laid down towels from the kitchen to Ant's bedroom and watched her TV until Billy's dad, Stan, got home. His sawdust-covered work boots left giant footprints in the carpet that filled with water. Sawdust and shit floated in the puddles left in his wake.

"This place needs a concrete foundation and hardwood floors," Stan said, swinging a claw hammer around his meaty index finger. Stan's idea was impossible: the house was a lima-bean green trailer up on cinder blocks—a mobile home that did not belong to them.

Ant said, "Just fix *this* for now." She always said this to Stan. There were boxes of unused collectibles and hand-me-down junk stacked around the house, and every bit of clutter had, at one time, been addressed with this command. Still, it remained.

But this day, Stan went out to the front yard, found the septic tank markers, and dug into the hard, red dirt until he had formed a basin around a slender black pipe with a valve at the top. He released the valve. Whatever pressure had forced the old shit into the house now released it out of the pipe and into the yard, filling the earthen basin until it became a putrid, shit-filled pond; a swarm of flies gathered immediately over the water and mosquito larvae began to multiply uncontrollably. The pipe coughed up wads of stringy old paper, sinking into the water with a plop, only to reappear floating, pulled apart and trailing across the surface like fake spider-web. The shit was probably not all theirs—some surely belonged to former tenants, and had been stored in the rusty old pipes and murky limits of the tank as memories are shuttled off to the dark corners of the brain—but it seeped out into what was now their yard, and it was entirely their problem. The sudden excess of water and crumbly shit was sucked up by the crusty, hard land, filled for years and years by pine needles that would not decompose, would not give up nutrients to earth so stale it had no choice but to drink up septic water as if it were lapping at a wholesome fountain of youth. Billy's parents had tried growing a vegetable garden, but all that mountain soil ever yielded was hard tomatoes and wilted broccoli. Now they grew shit.

After a few days, the water began to flow out of the basin and throughout the front yard, until even the gravel driveway squished when stepped on, as if the whole quarter acre were sitting on top of a sponge. When a car pulled into the driveway, the whole yard shifted and sloshed like a waterbed. The septic would have to be replaced, but it was expensive, and they had no help from their landlord.

They lived in Paradise, California, but a tour of their small lot would make you think they lived on a farm in Wyoming, which was in fact was their dream. Paradise had been their dream once too, back when they lived in Tracy and Stan worked graveyard at the box plant; but now paradise had turned into Wyoming while Paradise was flooded with shit. To simulate Wyoming, they tried to squeeze a farm onto their quarter-acre rental lot by stuffing it with themselves, Billy, three dogs, nine cats, six chickens, four geese, two goats, and a cow. The cats were various degrees of stray, the dogs stayed strictly in the back but were let in at night, the chickens fought with the geese in a shit-splattered coop in the corner of the front yard, while the goats and cow lived on either side of the mobile in their own too-small pens, built by Stan's hands with leftover lumber

10

from Meeks, where he drove a truck. The cow was still a baby, gotten after they had slaughtered the pigs the spring before. All of this Wyoming in California meant that, when their septic tank exploded into their house and yard, they couldn't call their landlord for fear of being evicted.

Stan used a Shop-Vac to suck up most of the water from the carpet, but the smell still hung in the air, a smell of old water at the bottom of a well, a smell like the wisp of a fart filtering from the room, a smell that hung around and mixed with Ant's potpourri, or that of a cooking dinner, to make an entirely new smell, like shit lasagna or a bouquet of shit roses. Everything they ate tasted like shit, everywhere they went, they were sure they smelled like shit. For a long while in the beginning, they sat around with their noses pinched in clothespins, but, slowly and unnoticeably, they grew used to it: Ant no longer stopped in the corner of the grocery store to sniff herself, and she no longer dabbed Billy with Stan's cologne before letting him leave for school; Stan, who worked in the sun and sweated and stunk like a mule anyway, was never bothered by thoughts of carrying the shit stink with him. They had come to a point, collectively and without speaking of it, where they believed that if they had to smell like shit, so be it. The yard was the big problem now, and it would require hiring a septic specialist to come and dig out the old tank and replace it.

Ant got a job taking care of a couple of old fogies down in Chico, and had to stay with them until after dark. Stan started going to the dairy farms after work to see if they needed help running their milk tankers in the winter—with persistence, but little luck. It was October and most of the tankers had drivers already. Still, Stan came home late after waiting on the edges of farms on the off-chance of work, digging his toe into gravel like a boy waiting to be picked for schoolyard baseball, and so it was up to Billy to get the fire going when he got home from school and make sure all the animals were fed. He would do this and, once it got dark, turn on the TV in his room and look out the window, waiting for one of his parents to come squishing into the driveway.

He came straight home after school, which was no problem, because he had no friends. Besides, if the goats got too hungry, they would start bleating like crazy. Neighbors had complained, threatened to call the landlord. Nothing had been done yet. Billy learned that when one of their neighbors came knocking at the tall front gate to ignore them. They always wanted to come in and brought with them all sorts of questions

11

about his parents and where they were and how they could leave such a young boy home all alone. If he heard a knock, or if the phone rang, he turned out his light, turned the TV off, and lay on his bed. Alone in the dark, the septic smell became the entire world. He imagined that stale stink of piss and shit moving through the house as visible as snow in the wind, climbing through his nose and into his lungs, filling his bladder and stomach again, so that all he would eat and breathe and drink was distilled piss and shit, and he would piss and shit it out again, and it would go right out the toilet and into the front yard to rise up into the air. He was learning about the water cycle at school, about how the world moved only in circles—every toilet flush became a gurgling splash in the yard, confirming this.

Now it was mid-November. Billy was home from school, about to feed the goats. Heavy clouds, black and grey, were boiling quietly overhead. The pine trees around their yard stuck up like black sticks, scraggly and jagged. Stan had dropped a big pile of alfalfa hay in the driveway the night before, so Billy went out to it and gathered up two big handfuls, pressing them against his chest. Dry flakes of the dense, stringy hay stuck to his sweatshirt and his nose filled with the green dust. He used to let his nose fill with the flakes to cover up the shit, but at this point it wasn't the smell that got to him, it was how the soggy ground slid beneath his feet, the way one step made the gravel ripple and rupture, a thick, black sludge oozing from secret pockets hiding just beneath the driveway surface. He imagined that any day now the shit would start poking up through the ground like clover, toilet paper would open and flower like dandelions. He breathed in as much of the scent as he could, and walked quickly, making his way towards the goat pen on the other side of the shit pipe and its dark pond.

As he was walking by the shit pipe, trying not to look at it, he heard a sudden, vaporous gasp, followed by a gurgle; a thick gust of wind, foul with the smell of old toilet water and fresh shit, came rushing over him. The smell—so fresh, as if a ragged shit had been smeared beneath his nose—penetrated even through the hay. It was as if he had smelled shit again for the first time. He gagged, bent over, and spat strings of thick vomit slime onto the ground.

It smelled as though a fresh shit had just been spat into the yard. But no one had been home all day. Old shit didn't normally come out during the day. Billy thought that all of the old shit was already in the yard, out in the open, floating beneath his bedroom window. He turned towards the smell. It was not a fresh stream of shit after all: rising slowly out of the water, dripping wet and blinking, was a tall pile of shit. Just a small mound at first, it kept rising up, growing taller and wider until it loomed above Billy, casting a long, dark shadow over him. For the most part it was an indefinable brown mass, but here and there individual logs and features stuck out: it clearly had a mouth, which opened and closed, lips smacking, releasing the same fart-smelling air with every breath. Its eyes were globules of toilet paper.

The great mound slid like a slug to the edge of the water. It moved slowly, its whole mass wobbling. "Do you have the time?" it asked.

"Four o'clock," Billy said. "Are you my poop?"

The pile laughed.

"Not entirely. Tell me, what year is it?"

"Nineteen-ninety four." Billy pressed the hay tighter and tighter against his chest. He stepped backwards. Though the shit was enormous and bubbling, it had no smell at all, save the dull and muggy stink that filled the house and that Billy had gotten used to.

"Ah," said the shit, and it leaned back, or appeared to: the shit that was its face slid up to the top of the pile, while the shit at the top rolled off, cascading down its great back, plinking and splattering into the water. Then its face slid back into place.

"Forty-five years!" said the shit.

Billy could say nothing. He was still amazed by how tall the shit was—easily two feet taller than him. If he had been as tall as the shit, he could play basketball at lunchtime with the older kids. They would pick him first, and they would all know his name.

"What are you?" he said finally.

"It's a long story," said the shit. Little bubbles were always popping all over the pile, making the dull squishing sound of moldy fruit hitting the floor. The dogs started barking in the backyard.

Billy stepped backwards again until he felt the jabbing end of a pine branch in his back. "I need to feed the goats," he said.

"Wait!" said the shit. "Don't you want to hear my story? I have so much to say!" Its eyes stretched out wide, until the toilet paper that formed them was thin and transparent; its mouth opened until it was as big as Billy was tall.

"Like what?" Billy asked, squinting into the windy, fetid yawn of the shit.

The shit gave a squirm, a sloppy twisting that shook turds from its sides and back like a dog shaking off water.

"Um…hey! Do you like to read?"

Billy took a step towards the goat pen.

"Because I've got a book," the shit said breathlessly. "Have I got the book for you!"

"Me?" Billy tried to point at himself—as if the shit wouldn't know who he meant—but his arms were full and tired from holding the thick bunches of hay.

"Yes, you! That is, if…" the shit looked around conspiratorially: it's eyes swished back and forth and all the shit from one side of its body swung to the other; great streams of brown sludge ran down its sides. Finally, its eyes settled in the middle again. It leaned dangerously over the edge of the water towards Billy. "…*If you want to live forever!*" it whispered loudly.

"You can live forever?" Billy dropped the hay.

The shit leaned back again, a smug smile on its face. "Apparently so, my friend. Apparently so."

"But you're poop." He gestured with his hay-dotted arms at the festering shit-field. His arms felt light, and for some reason, capable of anything—as if he could lift up a great pile of bricks, or push cars all by himself.

"Yeah, but I feel great!" The shit flexed like a bodybuilder.

Billy stepped towards the shit. He stood at the edge of the water. The shit smiled down at him. Up close, Billy could see the various colors of the shit—dark splotches here, raggedy brown speckles there—mysterious greens and impossibly whole chunks of food all over. It still had no smell, nothing more amazing than the tang of pine or the gathering whiff of rain. He reached towards the shit. His hand passed through the shit as if he were putting his hand into cold, cookie dough. It globbed onto his fingers, thick and sticky, yet wet, squishing loudly. When his arm was in up to his elbow, he felt the hard edge of a book. He grabbed it by the spine.

"There you go!" said the shit.

He pulled his arm out slowly, and as the pocket he had made refilled with air and shit, it made a squelching, farting sound. Both he and the shit laughed. His arm was completely covered in runny blobs of shit. He went to the hose, holding his arm and the shit-soaked book out away from him. One good spray from the hose cleaned everything off; he wouldn't even have to wash his sweatshirt, and the book was undamaged. He was near the corner of the house. He flipped the book open and glanced up at the shit, who had floated over to the nearest edge of the pond and was looking at him, its big smile and wide eyes shining between two branches of a small, black oak.

"Yes, yes," said the shit. "We never have to die!"

There were pictures in the book and lots of words. A slight wind picked up, crossing coldly over Billy's face with the terrible stink of shit. He gagged. His eyes watered. The goats started bleating from their little pen. The wind passed and again, there was no smell. He dropped the book and went to where he had left the hay.

"What are you doing?" said the shit.

"I have to feed the goats." He picked up chunks of the hay, stuffing them in his pockets and down the neck of his sweatshirt.

"Don't you want to learn how to never die? Aren't you afraid? I was afraid. I was so afraid of dying I looked everywhere to avoid it. Thank God I found this book! I've seen people die, and it is so painful. And then, you're gone. But this way, you never feel pain, you never go away. Have you ever seen anyone die?"

"Yes," Billy said. He thought first of his siblings—twins who had died—but that was before he was born. He thought next of the pigs: mean, sloppy animals, covered with mud, grunting, with little black eyes lowered and angry, who would charge Billy when he went to see them. To feed them, he had to stand on the porch and pour the feed over the fence into their pen. When they had been killed, a man had come from the butcher shop and brought the two muddy beasts out into the front yard. They weren't mean to him at all. It was raining and the pigs were covered with even more mud and shit than normal; they were almost black with it. The man dumped a pile of green pellets onto the ground and while the pigs rooted around for it, he pulled a rifle from his truck and shot one, and then the other, in the head. They squealed and kicked at the mud. He took a knife and slit their throats and blood pooled beneath the giant, writhing monsters, mixing with the muddy rain water and flowing out across the yard in dark, swirling rivers. Billy had watched from his bedroom window without once looking away. Yes, he never liked the pigs, and yes, it was terrible to watch them die, and he was sure that they hurt very much just before they were gone, maybe even while the butcher hung them up and cut their bellies and took all of their guts out into a pile in the dirt. But he was certain, also, that all the blood that flowed so freely down the driveway was still partly there—there had been too much to ever wash away completely. The shit was right; it would probably hurt to die. But when you were dead, you also didn't stink, or scare little boys who were only trying to be nice and feed you, and so when you were dead, all that little boy would have left of you was the dried blood in the driveway dirt and the memory of how sad he felt when he watched you die.

"What if everything changes when you die?" he asked.

"You a gambler?" laughed the shit.

"No," Billy sighed. "I have to feed the goats."

He went and fed the goats. He set the hay down in their trough and then stood in the center of their small pen, arms out straight, while both Lilly and Pearl circled around him, nibbling the bits of alfalfa off his sweatshirt with their nimble, purple tongues. Lilly licked his face for the green dust and followed the trail down his sweatshirt, pulling the sharp pieces from against his neck. Normally, this was Billy's favorite part of the day, letting the goats search him for food. They were gentle and warm, and would rest their foreheads on his when they were done and let him run his hands up and down their long, coarse necks. He thought about their heads, how when they were babies they had little nubs of horns. His dad had burnt them off. He told Billy to hold their baby goat legs while he pressed a red-hot iron against the horns. The little goats screamed and bleated and their legs pushed against Billy. He thought they would hate him like the pigs hated him, but with reason. A few minutes later, though, they were running all over the yard, jumping onto the deck with their clacking hooves and bleating playfully.

He felt a drop of rain on the top of his head. He looked up into the blackening sky, a white drop of water here and there streaking across. He gave Lilly and Pearl a final pat on the head and went back to the shit, picking up the shit's book on the way.

16

"You have to go away," he said to the shit. "My mom's coming home soon."

"She won't get home until after dark," said the shit.

"Still," said Billy. "You can't be in our front yard. You have to go back to where you belong."

"Your dad opened the septic tank. He released me," said the shit, sliding away a short distance. Then, quickly sliding back, "Have you ever heard of black magic?"

Billy looked up at the sky. "If it rains, will you wash away into the yard?"

"I hope not!" Something burst on the back of the pile, and shit sprayed the side of the house.

Billy sighed. "I have to go inside now. You should be careful."

As he walked away, the shit yelled after him, "This offer won't last forever, buddy, but I will!"

Billy went in and sat at the kitchen table, which was cluttered with a bunch of Ant's papers and files, stacks of Stan's old hunting magazines. The whole house was cluttered, and the whole back yard, too; wherever there wasn't an animal, there was some old piece of junk that his dad had dragged home from work. Billy pulled out his sketchbook and pencils from his backpack and pushed his mom's papers aside. One of her folders opened, exposing the edge of a picture that he knew without seeing. It was the only picture taken of his older brother and sister, Lucy and Travis. They had died in the hospital shortly after birth. In the picture, his mom's face was thin and sweaty, and her eyes were red and huge; Travis and Lucy, identical and premature, were still covered with goo and their eyes were squeezed shut and they were crying and tiny and pink. Billy had asked once which one was Travis, and Ant had gotten very quiet, and said she didn't know, and she had gone away into her room and didn't come out for a very long time. Billy closed the folder and put it at the edge of the table, far away from him. It was true, too, that when you died, you made everyone who knew you or who would have known you sad. He could hear the shit out in the yard singing softly to itself. It had the voice of an old crooner, and was singing a medley of Sinatra songs.

Outside, it was starting to rain. Billy began drawing a picture of the shit to show his parents when they got home. When he finished the shit, he opened the shit's magic book, flipping around for pictures. He found

17

a painting of Ponce de Leon standing on a rock and pointing to some jungle. Billy copied the explorer's picture onto his paper, next to the shit. Then he drew himself on the other side, what he hoped he looked like when he got older: tall, with big muscles, on top of a skateboard. Billy gave the shit two very long arms, and put one on his shoulder, and the other around the great Spanish explorer. He looked at the picture for a long time, for so long that when he closed his eyes he could still see the three of them together. Rain began to patter hard against the aluminum roof.

He put his hood up and went back out front and stood before the shit. It was almost completely dark, but the shit was half-covered in yellow porch light. Rain fell between them.

"*Mooooon Riverrrrr,*" the shit sang, looking away from Billy.

"How do you live forever?" Billy asked.

The shit faced him, not by turning, but by sucking its face through the pile until it slowly emerged on the other side, blinking away pieces of shit until it could see clearly. "First, you have to put your soul into a container," it said, turds falling from its mouth.

"Like a septic tank?" Billy asked, scrunching his nose up.

The shit sighed. "I would urge you to take longer to make your decision than I did. But, yes."

"What happened to your body?" Billy crossed his arms and held his shoulders. His legs were shaking.

"It rotted away. Most things do." The shit gave a kind of shrug, the pile bubbling and heaving up.

The rain fell and fell, forming little streams down the sloping gravel driveway, dripping in wide curtains from the edge of the roof. The sound of it was everywhere.

"But not your…soul? Do you have a soul?"

"Oh, yes. Yes, you have a soul, and it won't go anywhere, as long as you put it somewhere safe." Rain ran down the shit, taking big chunks of it along its wide mass, dropping with a familiar plunk into the shit-pond. The shit appeared to be growing smaller. One of its toilet paper eyes was running down its face in stretchy globs.

"That's what I thought," Billy said, kicking some gravel into the shit with a *plink*. He looked up at the dark sky through the pine trees. They made a kind of jagged circle, like a crown, filled with roiling grey and cold. "Why did you flood our house?"

The shit sunk with the slobbery sound of a deflating balloon, closed its eyes as if thinking. "Have you ever felt so trapped that your spine twists inside your body, just trying to pull out of your skin?" it asked quietly.

"Sometimes," Billy said, stepping eagerly forward to the edge of the shit, reaching out as it shrunk away to an unavoidable nothing, reaching out to keep it there, for just a moment longer, because suddenly he wanted to say just so many things.

In the Lightning

Thunder shook the house. Billy lay on his side, head pressed under the pillow, eyes wide on the window, which lit up every few minutes at random with a flood of crackling white light. The thunder cracked the sky then fizzled away, like a tree crashing to the ground in reverse, with the wide rattling of branches shrinking back to that first thin crack of the trunk. The dogs were barking furiously at the back door, and the bleating of the goats was high and full of murder, as if each blast of lightning was cutting right through them. Billy wanted to go out and see them. He wanted to crawl into their pen, slide across the wet and yellow hay and slip between them, into a breathing nest of fur and warmth. He wanted even to cross the hallway and knock on his parent's door, slide between them into the sandwich of their sheets. But he could not. He was frozen to his bed as if each strike of lightning were searching for him, and only through the utter stillness he had found in this curled position could he avoid it. Torrents of rain gasped while the lightning streaked and the thunder tore, and then came rushing down again in the inhaling silence afterwards.

He had just turned ten. Monkey Dunk, his small, grey-stuffed monkey, dressed in the light green pajamas Billy had worn home from the hospital after being born, had been put up in the closet after his birthday. He was too old now. Double digits. No one he knew older than ten still slept with stuffed animals. Not his mom, not his dad. He glanced towards the towering closet doors—an entire acre of room away, it seemed. He closed his eyes and pulled his blankets up over his head.

When he opened his eyes, expecting to see only darkness, more lightning flashed and he saw instead the pale white face, hidden behind strands of dark blonde hair, of Lucy. The lightning faded away, replaced by a shuddering peal of thunder, but Lucy was still there, warm in the darkness like a trapped breath. She looked exactly as he always thought she would: like their mother, only younger and thinner and smaller. Billy and his parents had brown eyes, but Lucy's were blue. Travis had probably had brown eyes too, but in Billy's mind he was blurry and grey. Lightning flashed again and Lucy smiled; Billy reached up towards her, the lightning fell away again and she was gone, save for a warmth at his fingertips. The dogs howled madly, running through the hall and skittering on the linoleum in the kitchen, but Billy could only hear the sound of his breath and the heavy silence of Lucy just at the edge of his sight and touch. He smelled burnt hair.

An instant later, a thick bolt of lightning broke down from the clouds and hung between heaven and earth in a shivering, twisting, and continuous bolt; around it danced blue flame—the whole night was lit up for one, long, minute. Everything was perfectly still. Nothing made any noise anywhere. Lucy was still smiling in the small warm pocket of space under the blankets—Billy smiled back. She was wearing nothing; her body seemed to be made of the stuff of his bed-sheets, white and milky in that eerie light, but her face was clear against the blue pillow, enfolded by a sweep of sheet at her chin. It was round and pretty, her face, but hidden by a mess of hair tangled as if she'd just gotten done playing a long game of hide-and-go-seek: disheveled from all those hours of being sought, and tired from keeping back giggles every time the searcher got close enough to touch. Billy just looked at her.

"Hey, Loose," he said.

"Hi, Billy," she said.

There was no noise at all, only Billy's breath lightly blowing, forming a semicircle of rumpled sheet just under his nose. The rain had stopped, and so had the lightning. He felt her holding him, a gentle stirring across his skin.

"You know me?" he asked.

"Yes," she said hurriedly. "I've seen everything you've done—I know you really good. I know how you daydream at school—I like the one about Bigfoot living behind the backstop in the playground. You can make macaroni and cheese all by yourself, and when Dad took the training wheels off your bike, you went off riding straight and didn't once fall over.

You are getting so old and big, Billy." She smiled, but it looked like how his mom—their mom—smiled when he said something to her and she was thinking of something else, something very far away.

He wanted to see what Lucy was thinking of now, he wanted to know that far away place—but he was very afraid. "I could show you how to ride a bike," he said.

She closed her eyes and it seemed to Billy that he could still see her eyeballs through the lids, searching back and forth. "Mmm," she said, "I would like that, but I don't think it would work. Thanks anyway."

"Do you want something to eat? You must be hungry."

She shook her head. Her eyes were open and filled with blue light. "I can't."

He rubbed his teeth over his bottom lip. "I-I wasn't sure."

"It's okay," she said, and it seemed—though Billy could see no arms or hands—that she held him ever tighter, coiling like a snake, warm and soft like a blanket on a Saturday morning. "I wouldn't want you to know."

Billy knew this about death: once, years ago, when he still carried Monkey Dunk with him, he had taken him to the park and left him by accident. Knowing somehow that this was the gravest mistake of his life, he raced back. The park had a tall red tower in the middle of a long sand pit; the tower had a ladder you could climb up and a pole you could slide down. It was Billy's favorite. But running back to the park looking for Monkey Dunk, the tower glowed blood-red in the sun, and the sand waved in a boiling mirage, and Billy could see, even from a distance, the spread and torn remains of his oldest friend littered about at the base of the tower. The monkey head was on the other side of the merry-go-round, hard plastic eyes scraped over with sand; his arms and shoulders were next to the pole, and his back trailed down from these, but his stomach was gone, and out from his stomach had been pulled every piece of stuffing inside of him; his legs were crossed a few feet away as if he were sitting in a lawn chair. Crying, Billy gathered them up, all the pieces one by one, cradling them in his arms, and carried them home.

And he knew this about death: Lucy, who was older than him, and Travis, who was Lucy's twin, had died when they were babies, had never made it home from the hospital. In the only picture there was of his older siblings, they were babies: in the instant flash of that one picture their entire life was captured. But in the long minute that sky and ground each held one side of a magnificent bolt of lightning, Lucy held him, as old and beautiful as she should have been; and Billy reached out and caught his breath, for he touched her, felt her right there, at the end of his hand; and in that instant the earth relented, and the bolt of lightning raced back into the clouds and left behind it the crackling boom of a thunderclap, and the house shuddered and shook, and mirrors broke and dressers fell to the ground in a spill of drawers and clothing; silverware clattered in the kitchen; the dogs screamed and tore through the house.

And then, a silence. And then, thousands of waiting raindrops, falling.

The Attendant

I.

Arthur Aggie fell in his garden while picking tomatoes and badly blackened his left eye. He tried to conceal it, but even a week later the purple bruise was still visible, snaking down his cheek like an exploded firework. His wife, Millicent, didn't notice because she was blind. He didn't see other people very often because neither he nor Millie left the house much: their groceries were delivered and they had long ago given over all socializing and work in the community to their daughter, Nadine, who would, in fact, be the one to finally notice her father's injury—when she had cleared some time from a busy schedule for her semi-regular visit. And she didn't notice until she had been there for two hours, because Arthur kept the apartment dark and she was wearing a black veil that hung from the wide brim of a black hat. It was typical of her style of dress—veils and pearls and lacy gloves—she had once remarked to a prominent professor at a cocktail party that the Aggies were the Kennedys of Chico, California, and she helped perpetuate the myth by carrying herself, in manner and dress, like the image of a Kennedy. She appeared to have no thought of removing her hat or her veil while visiting her parents—she never stayed long anyway—and, sipping tea on the couch in the dark, looked like someone who had just entered a funeral parlor. Millie was parked across the coffee table from her daughter, and Arthur sat in the corner in his leather wingback.

"And so I've decided to begin a scholarship fund in your name, Father, for—Father! Your eye!" Nadine screamed, her teacup clattering on the saucer. She put a gloved hand to her mouth. "What have they done to you!"

"Ah!" snarled Arthur. "Who is 'they,' you wretched brat? It was your mother who did this to me, that fat sea cow. She was reaching for a box of ornaments in the hall closet and elbowed me as I tried to support her colossal posterior from collapsing through the floor. It's nothing, she's already apologized."

"Mom?" Nadine turned to Millie, who hadn't stood from her wheelchair in fifteen years. Millie raised her head like an owl waking in the night atop a branch. She even said, "Who?" her lips remaining in an "O" and her sightless eyes roaming through the darkness of the room.

Nadine turned back to her father, a thin man shrinking into his chair, bald and fuming. His face was wrinkled and grey and his hands were coated with liver spots. Seeing her parents thus—bruised from the slightest fall, morbidly obese and consigned to a wheelchair—she saw their deterioration clearly for the first time, removed from the slow ebb of time that had carried them all, unnoticing, to this moment. And she realized something: it was high time she hired someone to care for her parents.

Nadine was much too busy running the Aggie Foundation to care for them herself; she was the manager of their legacy, not their nurse. Years ago she had moved them to their current house, a ground floor apartment in a quiet neighborhood on Vallombrosa, with a small yard shaded by a neighbor's willow tree. Now she would move them again, into the Sierra Sunrise Village, a convalescent hospital masked as a bustling community for the elderly—complete with a board game night, stretch classes, and every third Wednesday, a luau in the cafeteria. The Village overlooked a glittering man-made lake rife with sewage runoff, surrounded by an upper-class suburb—houses grey, flat, and modern—with wide windows aimed at the lake in a glaring display of the opulence within. Houses like these grew out of the untended weeds in north Chico, driving the pheasants and coyotes into the canyon; these subdivisions, in honor of their former tenants, boasted names like Pheasant Run Park and Coyote Terrace, and were filled with imported elms and sycamores and gel-haired teenagers meandering along the manicured cul-de-sacs in, of all things, Ford Explorers. Sierra Sunrise was another such misnomer, evoking thoughts of waking up to cool, majestic mornings on a mountaintop with an uninhibited view of the waking world, when really it was a long, flat-roofed, brick building surrounded by a parking lot and the sirens of ambulances arriving and departing.

Arthur objected vehemently to the move, but Millie, who hadn't spoken an original thought in years, took the change as she had taken everything since her blindness: with all the unresponsive vacancy of a potato. A woman who had once stood before the Chico City Council hammering her high heel against the table, to demand a permit for a sewing-bee float in the Pioneer Days Parade, was now a torpid lump of fatty flesh, was incontinent, diabetic, wheezy with congestive heart failure, and accustomed to being shuttled to and from the bathroom, covered with her own shit. She would agree to anything said to her with a vapid smile and the slow blinking of clouded eyes.

When they were first married, Arthur and Millicent were very similar people: passionate, religious, hard-working, intelligent, politically active. With the advancement of years, however, they had grown drastically opposite. Millie: grossly overweight, resigned to the fact that her plight was constant and irreversible. Arthur: bone-thin, irrespective of his failing health, saw no reason why he shouldn't be allowed to continue taking care of himself and his wife. In his mind, he was still the physical specimen that had served in the Army, spent twenty years coaching girls' basketball, and led summer camp youth-group hikes up Mt. Lassen. But, of course, he wasn't that man anymore: he was decrepit, arthritic and asthmatic, relying heavily on two replacement hips and a steel-reinforced walker to remain upright. Yet, because his mind was still as sharp as it had been thirty years before, he argued with Nadine for weeks that one little fall in the garden shouldn't lead to such drastic measures as giving up all control over their lives. And by control, of course, he meant hope. Nadine didn't see this, or what it meant to her father. While Millie's ailments and her lack of a grip on reality were obvious, Arthur's firebrand spirit and still-agile mind confused Nadine; she saw it not as his one remaining strength, but a further sign of his failing.

"The bruise is gone, Nadine," Arthur said the afternoon of the move.

"But you might fall again, Father," Nadine said, blowing the veil aside to get a better view of the packing tape in her hand.

"And I might smash your face in with my brass clock," Arthur spat. "It would certainly make the world a better place!"

Nadine sighed and shook her head. She pulled out a long stretch of packing tape and laid it across the flapping top of a box, humming *God Bless America*. She believed his outbursts were out of frustration with his inability to reason, to see that she was right, to understand his new role in the world. As the major figure behind the Aggie Foundation, Nadine was well-versed in Arthur's personal history, and nothing in that storied past would have suggested he would end up like this.

He had been a sweet man in his youth, working for years in a candy factory, arriving with pockets full of crunchy nougat at any gathering where he thought there might be children; he had been a schoolteacher and a volunteer fireman; an intellectual and an amateur poet; a quiet and thoughtful man, seemingly full of peace. To see him now, full of malevolence, caused Nadine both wonder and dismay. She reasoned that he must be harboring traces of senility in that once magnificent brain of his—but this was off the mark. The reason for Arthur's caustic behavior was that his mind had remained perfectly accurate, remembering every tenth-grade astronomy lecture he'd ever given, capable still of complex deductions and intrigued by the latest in news, both local and national. This perfectly accurate mind had observed his crumbling body and its limitations, and consequently regarded the world with a hate equivalent to his losses. He saw fingers frozen with arthritis that once moved gracefully across piano keys; he saw a robust face shriveling into a mottled and sour visage, as pitiable and easily bruised as a moldy peach. He felt age tightening around his joints in a cold, steely vice. He saw short distances— as from his bed to the toilet—warping into an arduous ordeal that left him breathless, tired, and weak. Arthur's anger bubbled out from a crystal-clear awareness of his mortality, from a clouded and aimless resentment: whom can you blame, with satisfaction, for the ravages of time? Nadine believed it came from denial, and had used accounts of his rash behavior to expedite her parents' inclusion into the Sierra Sunrise Family. And so, when Arthur was forced to move from his home, where at least he could simulate vitality through self-reliance, he turned his powerful bitterness and all its unfocused resentment, towards Nadine. It would be her, and her efforts, her decisions, her every move that would take the blame for Arthur's current state.

Throughout the move he hobbled after Nadine and around her hired movers, slowly circling the boxes of his life they'd stacked around the house, standing weakly aside as they carted his collections of geodes and scientific equipment out to a rumbling moving truck. She paid him little notice, stepping away from him, ignoring his glares and screams and instructing the movers how to pack her parent's belongings and where to put them. Millie sat on the back porch overlooking the garden, carrying on a sporadic conversation with the hummingbirds she could hear fluttering at the feeder. Arthur, like everyone else, ignored her. He went after Nadine.

"Let me tell you a story, my darling!" Arthur shrieked from the hallway, spit dribbling down his purple lips. Nadine was in the living room looking at her checklist—three boxes of dishes were stacked between them, partially blocking his view, but he was too exhausted to move around them. "It's the story of a how a little girl lost her inheritance. Once upon a time there was a girl named Nadine Aggie, who was a terrible curse to her parents and put them away into a retirement home reeking of death and failed lives, and she thought she was going to inherit millions, but instead her wise and handsome father invested the money poorly but on purpose until he lost it all, and died with a fat smile on his face, laughing all the way to the grave! The end!"

Nadine looked up at him through the white summer veil she had worn for this laborious occasion. She tsked. "Father, this is what is best for you and Mother. Please, let me take care of you now, as you took care of me all those years."

"You were your mother's child, not mine," Arthur spat, banging his walker on the ground. The tennis balls affixed to its legs padded softly against the plush carpet. "I would have rather had a dog, but she was allergic. You were the compromise."

"Well, be that as it may," Nadine looked back down and made an emphatic check on her list, "I say you're moving, and so, you're moving. Besides, I have the power of attorney over your savings, so, if you'd like to make any investments, I would love to go over your portfolio with you."

Arthur could only narrow his eyes and flex his lips. His hands shook as he gripped his walker. A mover—a fat sweaty man with a thin mustache— picked up one of the boxes of dishes standing between Arthur and Nadine. When he had carried the box briskly out the door, Nadine was gone—fluttering off and checking her list, poking her head out the sliding glass door to say a word to her confused mother before gliding quickly away again.

As Nadine drove them across town to their new condo, followed by one of the moving trucks—the other was going to a storage shed that she had rented—she turned to Arthur, who was sitting beside her. She put a gloved hand against his cheek and sighed emotionally. "Father," she said with the dramatic trace of a Boston accent, "this is going to be the best thing for you. These people will take care of you, in this life and beyond."

"Beyond? What will they do? Put me on a canoe with all of my belongings and send me off across that shit-filled lake, to be stuck amongst the cattails, shat upon by sparrows? Will they sing battle-songs and hymns to carry me to Valhalla? I think not."

"I only meant that they will help ease you into the next life."

"Next life? My addle-brained fool, my head-up-her-ass dearie, this is it. There is no 'next life.' There is only one, and this is its wretched conclusion."

"Father…"

"Father nothing!"

"You have to believe—"

"I believe nothing. I am a man of science. One day, my heart will stop beating and I will die. It will be terrible. My bowels will empty into my bed-sheets, my stomach will become distended with fluids—not the least of which will be a healthy amount of morphine, because the pain of dying will have been so unbearable. For days I will have been incapacitated, drooling all over myself and my bed, making all manner of ungodly noises as my body, wracked with pain and in the throes of defeat, begs for drugs. Stand before me all you like, but I will ask only for morphine. Bring your chaplain to read my final rights, and have him douse my forehead with morphine. What is beyond *this*, Nadine, is the drug. Morphine is the final accountant of our miserable lives, not St. Peter at his Pearly Gates."

"You're upsetting mother!"

"Millie, am I upsetting you?" Arthur lowered the visor in front of him, and aimed the vanity mirror into the backseat, where Millie could be seen strapped in next to her wheelchair, fat rolling over the seatbelt, her limp smile aimed out the window.

"I've baked a pie for Mrs. Dougherty. She hasn't been feeling well, you know," said Millie.

"Precisely," said Arthur, flipping the visor back up. The sun pouring through the cypress trees blinded him, but he could not bear lowering the visor again and having his peripheral vision filled with the sight of his demented wife. "Nadine, your gift is not a gift at all: it is a robbery."

Nadine gripped the steering wheel hard. "I only want to give you the best care possible. You deserve it! You both do. You have given so much to this town, let it now take care of you. Not many people get this chance. So many people end their lives alone and in pain; you both will have the most attentive care that money can buy, you will be comfortable, and surrounded by friends."

"Friends? My friends are dead, and there is no kumbaya-singing reunion planned in the hereafter."

"You'll make friends—people your age. It will certainly be easy. I'm sure everyone your age will know who you are. You're the *Aggies*, for God's sake!"

Arthur turned to her, wheezing and sour. "No, for *your* sake we're *the* Aggies."

Nadine said nothing.

Arthur stared forward again. He was sweating, and his breath rumbled uneasily in his sagging lungs like a shaken spray can. He turned his pain into a grimace, and hoped Nadine thought his silence was muted anger instead of frail exhaustion. By "beyond," she'd most certainly meant that the Aggie Legacy would remain intact. "These people" were mere nurses; they couldn't usher Arthur into some eternal Paradise, and Nadine knew this. The only thing beyond Arthur Aggie's earthly life was his legacy and whatever "it" was included Nadine, for she was the caretaker and sole-inheritor of this legacy, and "its" only true convert.

Was "it" money, or years of community service, or his family—what had he done in life that had become this commodity his daughter peddled around town? There was the Aggie Library, the Chico High Vikings played on Arthur Aggie Field, and ground had recently been broken on the Millicent Aggie Memorial Playground. Surely, money had been made during their lives here in Chico, but what else? When Arthur and Millie first arrived, it was a small cow-town in the north valley. Yes, they had been there for all of its quickening growth, but had they been responsible for any of it? He had served on the city council, they had both been teachers, and they had been in on the ground floor of many, it turned out, wise investments; but had the Aggie name really been anything before

30

Nadine began to make it into something? She talked always of their Legacy, lasting deep into those hazy yellow ages to come—and yet here she was, carting them away and against their will, to be forgotten even as they lived and breathed.

They turned off Vallombrosa, a road shaded by the great trees of Bidwell Park, onto Centennial Avenue, and finally onto Bruce, which wound out of old Chico into those dry and weedy fields where their new home had blossomed from the dirt. As the road turned a corner around a fly-ridden horse stable and its blinder-eyed, feed-bagged residents swishing their lazy tails in the sun and muck, Arthur decided that it didn't matter what his legacy was, what it was that he left behind, because he was going to start a new legacy, one that would supersede all things he had done before: he was going to become, without a doubt, the meanest son-of-a-bitch who'd ever lived. And when Nadine tried to open an Aggie Museum or when she lobbied for new city policy using the Aggie name, or when she went looking for investors for some other ridiculous idea of hers, she would wilt in the cold-hearted specter of her father, who would henceforth be known only for his cruelty.

He began at once. He hobbled through the automatic doors of the Village—Nadine pushing Millie along beside him and a team of movers readying their belongings behind them. The general manager greeted them with a spray of flowers and a whole coterie of smiling employees.

"Mr. and Mrs. Aggie, it is an honor and a pleasure to welcome you to your new home!" said the manager, his box-shaped mustache stuck like a leech to his curling lips.

"Kiss my wrinkled ass, you fat wop," Arthur shouted. "In the War, I stabbed a dago who looked just like you in his fat throat, and when he begged for mercy, choking on my bayonet, I spat in his eye. People say they hate war, sir, but that was the happiest moment of my long and miserable life."

The general manager, Mr. De Silva, not knowing that this tale was a fabrication, that Arthur had served only briefly in the Pacific Theatre before being discharged with myopia, could only step back in horror. He dropped the flower spray. "Um…" he looked to Nadine, barking a false laugh. "That's…"

They all stood there in the afternoon sunshine falling across the parking lot, the automatic doors choking around Millie and Nadine, frozen in the doorway, as Arthur pushed his way through the stunned group of employees. He laughed all the way down the hall.

The nurses at Sierra Sunrise, caring or knowing nothing of the Arthur who moved to Chico from the destroyed bunkers of Pearl Harbor, who had worked in a candy factory and taught high school science and girls' basketball, who was an active member of the church and who had survived the Great Depression, knew him only as the Devil in Room 11A. Over the next several months, he ran off every nurse and personal care-giver on staff at the Village, until Mr. De Silva had a private meeting with Nadine informing her that they would no longer be providing in-house care for Arthur Aggie, because no one, not one kind soul who worked there, would suffer his abuse. He could remain in residency, and participate in activities—because she agreed to continue paying the outrageous monthly rent—but under no circumstances would a nurse or attendant step foot into his room again, unless the old bastard died.

Nadine, faced with no other options, put an ad in the paper.

II.

Ant was walking down Main Street, looking in the windows of all the downtown shops for "Help Wanted" signs. It was the fifth of October. Leaves were withering on the branch and falling to the street in crunchy drifts, piling in the gutters. Cold falls became lean winters, and when Stan didn't find an extra job, the winters were very tough. It wasn't looking good now; he was having little success even getting his regular hours at Meeks, and there was talk of lay-offs. To add to this seasonal stress, they had a yard full of shit—and not Stan's normal, junkyard, pack-rat shit—real shit, puddles and fields of shit shooting right up out of the ground. They needed extra money, and so here was Ant, looking for work in Chico, for what would be her first job since her first pregnancy.

It was the fifth of October. She stopped in front of Bird in Hand, a toy shop renowned for their yo-yo's. The window was filled with colorful kites left over from summer. They were on sale. There was a large one, red and orange, fashioned like a phoenix, swooping from the ceiling towards the glass, over a display with two baby-dolls reading storybooks to a barnyard play-set and a remote control race track. It was the fifth of

October, and in ten days her oldest children would have been twelve. She couldn't take her eyes from the baby-dolls. They were just like little people, sitting above those animals like caretakers. Their clothes hung from them like hand-me-downs. They must have been boy and girl: one wore tiny overalls and the other a skirt, and though they had the same faces and expressions, one had a slight curl of blond hair—just one strand—pinned to her forehead with a pink ribbon. Both had big, rosy smiles, with glass eyes that bobbled in their heads, looking not at the books taped to their hands, but out the window, low and across the street, and almost, if she knelt down and moved to the side, at Ant. Face to face with the dolls, she remembered what a family used to look like to her, before she had one. She'd always imagined that she would spend her day chasing her children around, buying them gifts, preparing snacks; but the image that presided over all others was of her stooping over to pick up fallen dolls. She imagined several children for herself, and for each of these children a whole array of toys, of googly-eyed and plush companions that would fill those young imaginations, would accompany them on voyages and be the keepers of secrets and the blueprints for future friendships. And she always saw the dolls as the unfortunate victims of her imaginary children's whims, their mood swings and changing pleasures, dropped and forgotten in a moment of carefree joy—and in Ant's mind the general mood of her family had always been carefree joy—and all through the house would be those open blue eyes and ever-smiling faces of discarded toys. Throughout the rooms of this imaginary house, Ant followed her children at a distance, picking the dolls up and putting them somewhere safe, in case they were needed again.

This, to Ant, was what childhood looked like. It was how she thought it would be to raise her own children. Looking at these dolls now, she felt like she could not conjure up one single image of what it looked like to raise children. The dolls flickered in front of her like a black and white silent movie; dated and yellowed pictures covered with dust. She felt like an utter failure. Billy had toys—he had Monkey Dunk and he had various dragons and monsters and action figures—but somehow, it didn't all pile up into the image of childhood that she had imagined. She remembered her sister and herself running through their grandparents' apple orchard with their rag-dolls, looking for shade in the deep irrigation ruts, kicking worm-filled and rotted apples across the brittle and dry summer ground. That was a childhood. Billy had a stuffed monkey with whom he had various adventures—they had been to the Moon, Mars, a magical kingdom, and even once to Africa to find Monkey Dunk's parents (they were millionaires)—but to have these adventures Billy carried his toy around their small yard alone, wandering back and forth in circles. She sighed.

A saleswoman appeared in the window on the other side of the dolls, smiling at her in a way that said, *Come in or leave.* There was no "Help Wanted" sign in the window, so she left.

She went home, defeated again, and waited for Billy to get home from school. She fed the goats and avoided the shit-field. She watched TV. The house was a mess, but she couldn't bring herself to clean it. Dishes piled in the sink, the shag carpet went un-vacuumed, dust gathered on the bookshelves. The shit smell still lingered a bit, but less when the house was dirty than when it was clean, because the shit had a habit of settling beneath the rest of the dirt and muck in the house. There was the smell, however, of dirty dog hair—petting the dogs left your fingertips black and knuckles smeared with hair—and cat piss and rotting food. There was an old ice cream bucket filled with watermelon rinds and eggshells under the sink, composting for the garden, forgotten, because where the garden was supposed to be was now a shit-field. The house was filled with junk, too, boxes of crap she and Stan had collected throughout their unstable lives; so much junk that the living room was filled with boxes, couches piled up with old lamps and broken VCR's. The dinner table, too, was piled with magazines and folders and rusted silver platters, so they ate dinner in their bedrooms. Each bedroom had its own aged and unreliable television. She had imagined a family littered with toys, with dolls staring up from whatever arbitrary place they'd been dropped in favor of some other spontaneous enjoyment. All that was abandoned to the floor now were the various scraps of ideas and plans she had never followed through. So unbearable was the sight of her house that she couldn't bring herself to clean it, couldn't bring herself to care.

When Billy came home, he lingered for awhile in the kitchen, opening the refrigerator and the cupboards looking for a snack. Ant sat on her bed with the lights out, listening to the opening doors, the slamming shut, the vibrating emptiness within. The television was off and the curtains closed. Her room was completely dark. Billy kept opening cupboards, opening and closing listlessly, as if at some point, whether through magical intervention or desperation, new contents might appear, something tasty and desirable— or at least whatever was in there might conjure itself into something a gnawing stomach would find sufficient. Finally, he stopped, and after a few beeping sounds, the microwave roared to life. Then it was done, and a fork clinked onto a plate, and Billy's feet padded towards his bedroom and his door closed; the muted sounds of a television came through the door. Ant rolled onto her side and wept.

By the time Stan came home, darkness had fallen completely and the fall chill settled through the house. The only light on was the one from Billy's television—a thin line of blue at the base of his door. There was no fire in the fireplace, no wood had been brought in. Ant was lying on her side, still, staring up at the ceiling. Stan's shadowy figure appeared in the doorway. He stunk of sweat and sawdust. He stood there for an entire minute, breathing loudly, before turning around and walking outside. A light turned on in the backyard, and Ant could hear the sound of an ax thudding against a block of wood. Then Stan walked heavily through the door, and a clatter of wood fell into the creaking wood-box. Billy's door opened. Ant could hear them talking quietly beneath the sound of Stan's hatchet easing slivers of kindling from a hunk of pitch-pine. Then, the gasping roar of a fire consuming newspaper, and the popping splat of pitch taking flame: slowly, heat snaked through the house.

Stan came to the doorway again, little bits of wood were stuck to his grey, sweat-stained shirt, illuminated by kitchen light. He rubbed at his beard. "Hey, we're thinking of ordering a pizza," he said.

"We have no money!" Ant moaned.

"We have no food either, honey."

She rolled onto her back. "Did you go by any of the dairies today?"

He shook his head. "Mike went by last night, said everything was filled up for good for the winter. I'll try Builder's Supply, sometimes they have deliveries on the weekends and their own guys don't want 'em. Did you look?"

She nodded. "All day. I couldn't find anything. Everywhere I went, they wanted two years of experience. I haven't had two years of experience in my entire life!"

Stan sat next to her, rubbed her thigh. "It's alright. We'll figure something out."

Ant turned onto her side again, her back to Stan. "I want pepperoni and olives, if you're getting pizza."

"Sure."

"And how are we paying for this?"

Stan shrugged. "I'll charge it, I guess."

"Oh, God!" Ant cried. "I wanted baby-dolls in our walkways, Stan, and now we're charging pizza!"

"Ant, honey, I have no idea what that means."

"Of course not."

But they left it at that, and Stan ordered the pizza, and when it came, Ant emerged, bleary eyed and tussle-haired from the bedroom.

"How was school, Billy?" she asked.

"Fine," he said.

"And work, Stan?"

"It was work," he said.

They each took two slices of pizza, and went to their rooms, and turned on their TVs.

III.

It was the sixth of October, and Stan had already left for work in the truck he had borrowed from Meeks. The lumber yard was in Chico, and because the Wrights had only one car between them, Stan's bosses would sometimes let him end his day with a delivery up in Paradise so he could keep the truck for the night. The sun wasn't up yet, but Ant was, and she was getting a fire going before she went out again, into the long defeat of looking for work. She was wadding up old newspaper into balls and cones and laying them around a pyramid of kindling and small blocks of wood. She lit a match: it withered out and died. She threw it into the woodstove and lit another one, and in its quick flare-up she saw a word, "HELP", in big, bold letters, written out at the bottom of one of the pages she had put in the fire. She let the match die and pulled out the page and unwrinkled it, laying it flat on the floor.

It was a full-page ad, half picture and half words. The words said: *The Aggies, pillars of the Chico Community, are looking for a personal caregiver to help them with day-to-day activities and chores. Wage: competitive.*

Hours: Daily, 7 am to 7 pm, and it had a phone number. The picture was of Nadine Aggie, in a pastel pant-suit with a pair of scissors, cutting the ribbon at the Millicent Aggie Memorial Playground; the hanging boughs of two oak trees filled out the top of the picture.

The date at the top of the page was from the week before, but Ant figured it was worth a try. So, a few hours later, when she had gotten Billy off to school, she sat down and called Nadine Aggie. Ant knew of the Aggies, of course—though she would have called them *one-time* pillars of the community. When she was a teenager, Arthur Aggie had been on the city council. He and his wife had infamously tried to promote a ban on Halloween in Chico—to cut down on the rowdy parties of the fraternities. But—and she could blame this partly on the fact that she rarely read the news; they only collected old newspapers from their neighbors to start fires—she hadn't heard the Aggie name in a long time, and had, without much thought, figured they died years ago. Well, if they were alive, then good for them—if it meant Ant could land a job out of it.

"Hello?" Nadine's voice rang across the phone line. Ant thought she detected a British accent.

"Um? Hello? Is this Nadine Aggie?"

"Why, yes it is. Who may I ask is calling?"

"My name is Ant Wright, and I'm calling about the job you posted in the paper. Is it still available?"

There was a muffled pause on the other end. "Oh, my, God, yes! Yes, it's still available. Very much so. Very much available. Today, even."

"Okay," Ant said.

"I can interview you right now, if you have time."

"Well," Ant said.

"Are you busy? Please don't be busy."

"Okay"

"Have you worked with the elderly before?"

"Well," Ant said, "When I was in high school I washed dishes at a convalescent home. I mean, yes. I dealt with the elderly."

"Dealt with? Oh, yes. Do you feel it qualified you for this position? What have you done since high school?"

"Well, I've taken care of my idiot husband and my ten year old son. So, I mean…a couple of old farts can't be any worse than that, right?" Ant laughed.

Dead silence answered her. Then a sharp, if forced, laugh. "Ha, HA! Yes, of course. My parents, my wonderful parents, I'm sure, are no worse than your husband and son. Better, even. Maybe even better than your husband and son."

"Okay."

"Do you want the job?"

"How much does it pay again? The ad doesn't say."

"Seven dollars an hour."

"Well," Ant said.

"Eight."

"Sure," Ant said, standing, heart racing. She realized that she had been holding a pencil in her hand, and that she had snapped it into bits at some point during the conversation. "Sure, I'll take the job."

"Can you start today?"

Within the hour, Ant was dressed in her finest muumuu—black with pink polka dots and a sweep of pink lace at the collar—and driving down to Chico in her red Jeep Cherokee. She was singing along to George Strait: "*I've got ocean front property in Ar-i-zo-na...*" It was cold outside, and trails of fog were clinging to the mountains, but a dimly yellow sun hung over the valley, and clouds of brown smog wavered up into the white sky. It wasn't warm necessarily, but it wasn't cold; in fact, it was perfect non-weather, weather that didn't affect you one or way another, as if you weren't even outside or anywhere in particular. And yet, somehow, Ant was happy. It was October the sixth, and in nine days, her oldest children would have been twelve, and she didn't once think about them.

IV.

Nadine met her at the front door. A thin woman, Nadine, with perky tits pushed up towards her chin, gaudy pearls strung around her neck and a clear veil hanging from a black hat—a beauty mark on her lip?—she extended a gloved hand to Ant, wrist up, a giant diamond shining from her slim finger. Was Ant supposed to kiss her hand? Maybe if she was the Queen of merry-old-England, Ant thought, and shook the hand by its dangling fingers.

Nadine's lips pursed behind her veil. "Well, my, hello, you must be…"

"Ant Wright. Call me Ant." Next to Nadine she felt decidedly like a whale: a bulbous and flowing behemoth meant for the gravity-free confines of the sea; her tits were enormous and sagging across her large belly; her ankles went straight down into her tube socks and sneakers caked with mud and goat-shit; she wore no jewelry or make-up—her most extravagant adornment being a white scrunchy pulling her long, wispy brown hair from her forehead—which, next to Nadine's fancy hat and veil, shadowing all but the impression of the beauty beneath it, she felt was as big as a ping-pong table.

"Ant! Oh, my, why on earth would I call you that?"

"It's my name," Ant shrugged.

Nadine folded her hands at her pelvis and made a squeaky sound. "So it is," she said chirpily. "Aren't you adorable?" she winked.

"Yeah," Ant said.

Nadine led her inside the Village, walking quickly past the front desk, where a young receptionist watched them pityingly. Ant thought it was weird, but, then again, the entire place was a little weird. Right through the front doors was a large dining area, surrounded by steaming buffet carts and a very slow-moving line of elderly people shuffling from station to station; here, a young Latino boy shoveled scrambled eggs onto a plate, there a young Latina girl drizzled gravy onto biscuits. A maitre'd in a loud red vest seemed to be seating the residents, helping them with a stout elbow into their seats. Half the diners stared vacantly into space, their white hair frazzled—if they had hair at all—their faces taut, revealing the contours of the skeleton ascending into being through that thinning skin; or else the skin hung from them in layers of wrinkles, their eyes roaming madly in confusion. The entire room echoed not with the hum of conversation or the scraping sounds of utensils on plates, but with the wheezy breathings of oxygen machines, the slithering stomp of walkers, and the drone of motorized wheelchairs. The air smelled like embalming fluid and sausage.

Nadine continued past the dining area with her brisk walk, Ant struggling to keep up. Mercifully, the Aggie apartment was just at the end of the hall on the first floor—Nadine waited there for a breathless Ant to reach her.

"Mother and Dad are at breakfast right now, so I can acclimate you to their apartment."

Ant felt as though Nadine were the nurse prepping her for the doctor; she followed her in. It was a small apartment, the door opening into the kitchen, which had a bar counter that looked into the small living room. On either side of the living room were bedrooms—Arthur's on the left, Millie's on the right—each had its own bathroom. At the end of the living room was a window, a balcony covered with potted plants, overlooking a trail that wound around the lake. The trail was dotted with stone benches, which were prime duck-feeding locations and thus coated with duck-shit. There was a green leather couch and a TV in the living room, an ornate glass coffee table with an inlaid carving of Chinese warriors, porcelain vases at each end of the couch, and the walls were covered with paintings, each a different motif—Tibet, Chile, Ghana (Nadine explained, in excruciating detail, the amazing origin of each imported painting).

"This one, from Japan, was given to my father by a man who had fought against the Americans in World War II," Nadine pointed to a scroll hanging in the hallway, just outside Arthur's door. "They worked together at a science symposium long after the war, and became colleagues and the best of friends. Isn't that something? Doesn't it just warm your soul, to know that the human heart is capable of such forgiveness?"

"Oh, yeah," Ant said.

"Do you have much art in your home?" Nadine asked.

Ant laughed. "Um, sure. My husband, Stan, bought a painting of someone's German shepherd at a yard sale once."

"Marvelous," said Nadine. "Does he raise dogs?"

"No," Ant shook her head. "But it was only a quarter."

"I see. Well, this one, from Tibet…"

And she gave Ant a history of the paintings, and showed her all of the photographs of her parents throughout their illustrious lives. Here was Millicent Aggie marching for civil rights; here she was, tall and beautiful, her hair a dark and curly halo, her face perfectly pale and smooth, feeding wounded soldiers in Hawaii. There they were, standing in front of their first home, both slim and young, Arthur with a full head of hair and wiry glasses, chiseled and handsome in his fancy suit, a strong arm around the thin and shapely waist of his bride—and in her arms a small baby swaddled in a cream-colored blanket; behind them the house on East 1st Avenue: a cottage with a spire-shaped attic, and surrounding their perfect lawn a dense line of trees, maidenhair and linden, reaching up into the sky.

All these pictures, and more besides, were hanging all over the walls, on every wall, even in the kitchen and bathrooms. They had lived such amazing lives. Arthur, at Bumpus Hell atop Mt. Lassen, teaching children about sulfuric acid; Millie, teaching the immigrant Hmong children of Hamilton City how to read; at Niagara Falls; at the Coliseum in Rome; building houses in Peru; even lying on the beach in Southern California, the Aggies, on lounge chairs with books opened on their tanned chests, seemed active.

When they were done looking at all the pictures—getting a feel for who they were, as Nadine said—it was time to bring Arthur and Millie back from breakfast. Ant already felt tired. It had been thirteen years since she'd actually had a job, and she'd forgotten what it was like to be in the presence of an employer, the sensation that your every move was being weighed and calculated, that you had ceded control of your time, of your life, to someone else. And, having looked at all the accomplishments of the Aggies, she felt exhausted, not only because Nadine carried herself with a whirlwind of energy—an overly caffeinated cheerleader for her family's past—but the sheer thought of what the Aggies had done in their lives became a weight on Ant's shoulders: the thought of the travels, of the constant motion, in contrast with her own life, and how few interesting pictures or exotic paintings it amounted to; these heavy thoughts made her feel very small, and, yet, grossly huge. The worse she felt about herself, the more aware of her body she became, of its sagging heft, of the trickles of sweat between the folds of fat, of her back aching against gravity. And Nadine, surely Ant's senior by several years, was as chipper as ever.

"Mother and Dad will be so happy to meet you!"

This was a lie.

Ant looked for the Aggies in the nearly empty dining hall, and saw nothing close to that history of images she had seen in the apartment. It occurred to her that none of the pictures hanging from the walls had been taken in the last several decades. There was a slow trail of doddering olds being led from the dining room by nurses. Ant and Nadine weaved through them.

"Yoo-hoo! Mother! Father!" Nadine called, raising her arm in the air.

And there were Arthur and Millie Aggie, in the far corner, still seated at a table with plates in front of them, alone. Millie, fatter even than Ant, in her wheelchair still had her hair in the curled halo style of her youth, cut neatly around her head, and it was still mostly dark—but nothing else was recognizable. She wore a flowery dress that looked like it had been ripped apart and stitched back together to allow her in, and she wore heels so small her fat feet swallowed them up, calves sagging like frosting bags down to the unnaturally dainty and pointed toes. Arthur slouched in his seat, bald head wrinkled into a grimace, glasses with lenses as big as dinner plates magnifying cold, sharp eyes; a brown suit, spotty and stained, hung from his shaking bones. Ant felt almost like crying, seeing them there. She had created in her mind two vibrant and life-loving old people, still hopping around the world and doing good deeds, having dinner parties with their friends. She didn't consider the fact that, if this were the case, they wouldn't need her; after seeing something of the lives of the Aggies, this amounted to nothing less than witnessing their deaths.

There were bits of egg and half a sausage on Millie's chest. Her hands patted the table searching for more food. Her lips smacked toothlessly. Arthur's plate was clean, and he held a cup of black coffee in his shaking hands. Neither looked up as they approached the table.

"There's no more, you abominable walrus!" Arthur snapped at Millie. "You've had enough."

"Pudding?" said Millie.

"Mother, Dad, I would like you to meet your new attendant. I've just hired her today."

"Tell these no-good hoodlums who work here to put rat poison in our next meal. We'd like to die now," Arthur said, raising the coffee to his lips; it spilled across his collar.

"I'll do no such thing," said Nadine. "This is Mrs. Wright."

"Call me Ant."

"Yes. Yes, Ant. This is…Ant, your new personal caregiver."

"Tell her to shove this knife into my eye!" said Arthur.

"Arthur used to work in the candy factory," said Millie. Her roving hands found a napkin, which she proceeded to sop into a papery mash in her slobbering mouth. "I have never had such a happy Easter brunch."

"And how much of my money do you eat up, my ugly slave?" Arthur looked at Ant for the first time. He was holding a butter knife.

"Eight bucks an hour," Ant said.

"Good God, you blubbery rhinoceros!"

"Dad!"

"And you!" Arthur stood now, leaning on the table, his eyes, so large behind those glasses, narrowing down at Nadine. "I should have killed you when I had the chance!"

"Uh, Mr. Aggie?" Ant said, taking a slight step away from the family.

"So many quiet, peaceful nights I stood above your crib as you slept. Don't think I didn't know what power I had! Once, I held a pillow just above your sweet little mouth, and if I had known all the trouble you'd cause me, I'd have done it, smashed the life right out of your lungs! But I held back, thinking maybe I would luck out and crib death would take you, and I'd be off the hook. But oh, no! Not I. Not so fortunate, I. Now, though, now I will strike you down, smother you, finally, after all these years!"

"You can have your doves," Millie said. "My favorite bird has always been the bluebird."

Arthur lunged for Nadine, butter knife first. She stepped aside with a lady-like gasp, and Arthur toppled towards the floor. And Ant, moving faster than she ever thought possible—and to the surprise of everyone looking on—fell to her knees and caught the flimsy frame of Arthur Aggie. The butter knife scraped harmlessly across her shoulder. He was lighter than a sack of potatoes, and she lifted him back up and into his seat. He glowered at her.

"Who needs you?" he grumbled.

"Apparently, you do," Ant said.

Nadine sobbed behind her veil. Millie continued to search the table. Bits of napkin were stuck to her chest. The Village staff, pretending to be cleaning up after the meal, moved in tightening circles towards the drama with ears turned. Arthur wheezed heavily.

"Very well, then." he said. "Carry me back to my room. I shall have a nap."

V.

It was October the tenth. Life at the Wright house had turned quickly upside-down. Ant was gone early, leaving with Stan before dawn and not home until well after him. Billy, though only ten, was left alone in the mornings and for much of the afternoon, and was having to take on responsibilities that his parents hadn't yet planned to give him. Ant felt bad about it, but they were in a spot. She needed a job, and if she could even find anything else, it wasn't going to pay as well as the job with the Aggies.

And she certainly earned every penny. It was hard work. She tried to figure out what was the hardest part about her job, but there were so many terrible things. Each day she would make a list of what she had done, or had been done to her, ranking each activity on a scale of 1-10 on how horrible it was. Cleaning up after Millie was always somewhere in the top three.

Millicent Aggie had not had proper control over her bowels for at least a decade. Each of the four mornings Ant had worked there, she arrived to find that Millie had covered herself and her bed with shit. And not only was she incontinent, her body seemed to no longer produce waste whole—she sprayed it like a hippopotamus. It was completely liquid. The shit pooled behind her and dripped onto the floor. On particularly violent movements, it sprayed onto the wall behind her. It rendered undergarments meaningless. And apparently, since moving into the Village, she'd even less control.

Arthur taunted Ant from the doorway as she wiped and cleaned. "Ha! You see what she thinks of you? You're shit. You are no better than her shit. She never shit like that when we were alone, carefree and capable. No. No, she does it for you. You might not think she has all her mental faculties, but mark my words you gelatinous blob, she is cunning."

Arthur himself, though easier to care for—he could get himself to the bathroom and was capable of eating like a mostly normal human being—caused an entirely different kind of problem. He followed her and harassed her wherever she went. As she carried the soiled bed linens out the door to the special garbage closet (Ant decided that, in the future, she wasn't going to work in any place that had a special disposal unit for "soiled linens") Arthur called: "Your true calling is as breeding stock. Like a cow. You should be kept in a small pen and have your young force fed and hog-tied, so those of us who matter to society can eat them as a delicacy. Only then would you serve a real purpose."

As he said this, the door closed mercifully behind her. It was October the tenth, and in five days her oldest children would have been twelve years old. She took a slow breath and continued on. When Lupe, who worked at the front desk, passed her in the hall, Ant pretended it was the reeking, sagging sack of shit in her hand that caused the tears in her eyes. Most of Arthur's comments were mindless hatred, and she found a lot of it amusing; and yet, sometimes, he did hit his mark, and it could hurt worse than anything—but Ant would never allow him to know he'd gotten her. And, she felt she was winning: he was running out of insulting names. In the past day he'd called her a "blob" three times and various breeds of cattle seven times. He had no new material, and got flustered trying to come up with new barbs to stick her with. Soon, she thought, he would get tired, and with his only remaining purpose in life—to be a mean old dick—gone, he would, hopefully, die. But she certainly wouldn't show a weakness to him, because, if he continued to attack that wound, that nearly twelve year old wound, then she might accidentally knock him over and kill him. Old people fall over all the time, and things might certainly land on their heads and crush them. It didn't help to have these thoughts when she knew the entire staff at Sierra Sunrise would defend her.

And that created a whole other problem with her job: the state of Arthur Aggie. Millie…Millie was just a bag of shit that would say random things and slop food all over herself. Ant was convinced that her brain was stuck in some endless loop of happy holiday memories, and good for her, because who would want to face the reality she had? That was sad, surely, but Arthur—Arthur was evil, which was not only frustrating but confusing. And, looking at those pictures displayed everywhere in the apartment, she couldn't help but notice his soft eyes behind the glasses, the easy smile on his handsome face, the many scenes of him captured with children, teaching them earnestly, it seemed—for no picture taken of Arthur Aggie had the scent of photo-op in it, as did those of his daughter—Ant had taken to reading the paper again during the Aggie's long napping periods, and there was a good number of pictures—usually ads paid for by the younger Aggie herself—of Nadine involved in some charity, or giving some lecture on the history of Chico, or like the picture that was the ad for this very job, dedicating something to her parents. Ant thought, if Nadine dedicated some time to her still living parents, then she could get weekends off. The good-nature and involvement of the young Arthur seemed completely genuine. Why, then, had he become so black-hearted?

When she got back to the apartment, the door only opened partway. Something was blocking it. She thought: well, maybe the old shit fell and died after all. Her heart fluttered with hope. She pushed the door and it pushed back with an obstinate mutter; Ant thought it was possible that Arthur could be obstinate even in death, but took this as an unfortunate sign of life. She slid through the half-opened door, having to squeeze and rearrange her drooping breasts to push them through.

Arthur had gotten stuck in the corner behind the front door. His eyes were worse than he let on, Ant reasoned, because he would walk himself right into walls, and continue to urge his walker forward, as if the wall would fall away for him. This, though, was the first time he'd landed in a corner. He grunted stubbornly.

"Ah, well, looks like the old blind armadillo got himself stuck again, eh?" Ant laughed, coming through the doorway.

"I thought it was you, you fat sea cow. I was trying to run you down."

"Sea-cow? Like I haven't heard that one before. You think you could run me down, you tired old fart? I must weigh five times as much as you."

"Yes," Arthur said, "You must." He blinked dazedly at her.

Ant gently put a hand on his back and grabbed the front of the walker. He stopped moving as she turned him slowly around and set him into the hall again.

"There you go," she said, patting his shoulder.

"Well. So." And he shuffled off to his room and closed the door.

She checked on Millie, whom she had cleaned up, sprayed down, coated with baby-powder, and set in her wheelchair by the window while she washed and changed the bed. It was already a routine of theirs. Millie's hazy eyes looked out towards the lake. An old couple, wearing matching blue shirts and Bermuda shorts, walked around the lake vigorously. Their wrinkled skin was red and stretched looking. It was cold outside, but still, they walked in wide laps around the lake.

"See them crazy fucks out there?" Ant said, fluffing the pillow she had put behind Millie's back. She'd noticed the old girl slumped over most of the day; the pillow helped her at least appear more alert.

"It's probably very cold out there right now," Millie said.

Ant stopped fluffing. "Millie, honey, did you just have a coherent thought?"

"It's too bad they only had iceberg lettuce," Millie clucked sadly. "The salad would have been so much better with romaine. I'm so sorry."

Ant smiled. "That's okay," she said. She sat on the couch next to Millie and watched her. Her eyes were grey and thick with cataracts. She farted uncontrollably. Her cheeks sagged and her chin was warty. Outside, it was cold and overcast; the grey light through the window made the room muted and pale, quiet, and Millie's face was ashen. She held her chin up, sitting straight in her chair against the pillow. Her eyes flicked back and forth behind her gold-rimmed glasses. Her gummy lips turned in a smile. A clear shadow rose from her. It was only the faintest movement, like dust from a shaken blanket filtering back to the ground, but something stirred inside Millicent Aggie and stood. It was thin and beautiful, wearing a tight black dress; it arched its back at a narrow waist, turning on full hips and raising its slender arms. Millie's face was slack.

"Millie?" Ant said, leaning back into the couch and raising her hands as if to say, I want no part in this, I don't see this—yet it was there, a trick of the eye, maybe nothing more than refracting light or a passing cloud, but undeniably right there in front of her. And what was it? An impossibility, a daydream, a floating blind-spot dancing across the eye. Ant lowered her hands. The room was perfectly still and terribly cold.

Millie blinked, took a deep, gasping breath, chest rising and flaccid face growing taut, and farted, long, loud, and wet. The shadow was gone.

"I believe," Millie said, "It's time for breakfast."

Ant stood, pulled the curtains aside and looked out the window. There was the old couple again, power-walking back towards the Village.

"Yeah," Ant said, touching Millie's warm and doughy shoulder. "Looks like it is. Let's wipe your ass and get out of here."

VI.

She came home late and tired. It was dark. There was no light on the porch. No smoke rose from the chimney. The house was so cold her knuckles hurt.

"Stan? Billy?" She put her purse on the table. She turned on the kitchen light. A basket of unfolded laundry had fallen from the table to the floor and spilled. Dishes were stacked in the sink from the night before. In front of the woodstove was a block of pitch-pine surrounded by tiny flakes of wood and a hatchet. Inside the stove was a small stack of kindling, flakes hardly bigger than those on the ground, and wads of paper half-burnt.

She cut some thick pieces of kindling and stacked them on fresh paper. She lit the paper and after a minute a small flame had taken. It whooshed and crackled. A door opened.

Billy was standing in the hall, wrapped in a blanket. His face glowed white, hovering in the darkness, his black hair melted into shadow. His eyes were wide and glistening.

"Hey," Ant said. "Billy, what's wrong?"

"I couldn't get the fire going," he said quietly. He leaned against a bookshelf, looking down at the rising fire in the woodstove with a mixture of longing and disappointment. There was a slight scar just beneath his left eye from a fall long ago, and it seemed to beat like a heart, throbbing on his face and filled with black.

"That's okay," Ant said. "Where's your dad?"

He shrugged. "He never came home."

"You were all alone?"

He nodded.

"Well, why didn't you turn on a light?"

"Someone was knocking at the gate. They were yelling something about shit."

"Shit?"

"About smelling shit."

"God-damnit," Ant said, standing now. "Come here," she said, pulling Billy close to her. She rubbed his back. "You're so cold!"

He nodded into her stomach.

She looked around the dining room and kitchen, half in light, and half in dark. The small and growing fire. The table and chairs, the laundry on the floor, the junk stacked in boxes, all of it untouched and cold in the gloom as if this were a crime scene whose contents were frozen in place for the investigation. Nothing seemed to have been touched in days.

"It's okay," Ant said. "We're going to fix that septic tank, and you won't have to worry about it anymore, okay? And your dad is probably out looking for another job, or he found another one. So, its okay, okay? What do you want for dinner?"

Billy shrugged against her, lifted his arms and wrapped them around her waist. The blanket fell to the floor.

They ordered Chinese food. They were sitting on Ant's bed eating chow-mein and watching *The Simpsons* when Stan finally came home. Everything was dark except for the fire in the woodstove and the blue flickering television. He stood in the doorway and watched.

"Well?" Ant said over her fork.

"Well, what?"

"Where were you?" She looked up at him. His shoulders and knees were caked with dried white paint.

Stan looked at the ground. "There were some lay-offs at Meeks."

Ant twirled noodles around her fork. Billy had stopped eating. He watched his parents. "And?" she said.

"I got laid off."

"So where were you?"

"Tom Maxwell had some work for me and a couple of guys after work, paintin' this house he just built."

"Well. Is that steady? Does he have a job for you?" She set her plate aside. Billy picked his up and started to eat again.

Stan took off his John Deere hat, held it on his finger, looked at its front. "No. Just the one-time thing, under-the-table."

"What are we going to do, Stan?"

He sighed and came into the room, put his hat back on. He leaned against the dresser. "I don't know," he said.

"At least I have my job." She looked down into her lap. Hair fell across her face, hanging to the blanket spread across her lap. It blocked her view of Stan, and she was glad.

"I guess we're pretty lucky for that," Stan said.

"Yeah," Ant looked back up at the TV. Billy was silent and unmoving next to her. "I guess we are, aren't we?" she said.

VII.

Ant was holding Millie's leg up, aiming the detachable showerhead at the crease between her fluttering ass cheek and her blubbery thigh. The water sprayed out brown and sometimes chunky from the crevice. Another morning watching shit swirling down into the drain for Ant. What had she done? What had she gotten herself into? And all of this now with the pressure of being the sole breadwinner. It wasn't just to help them out anymore; they needed her to keep this job, to put up with Arthur's cruelty, to continue maintaining Millie, keeping her clean and dressed and for what? The crazy old coot lived only for her meals, only rose long enough from her stupor for a moment of lucidity dedicated to breakfast, lunch, and dinner. And then, after blindly slopping food across herself and the table, smacking loudly and gumming every bite into a slobbering paste, she dipped back down into the swirling fogs of her everyday, descended into that constant memory, that anywhere-but-here in the recesses of her mind to which she had retired long ago. What was the point?

It had been weeks since Stan was laid off, and he still hadn't found another job or any extra work. She had no idea what day it was. Ant herself had become lost in the routine of her two charges.

She toweled Millie down and pulled a dress onto her, shoved her feet into her shoes. She parked her wheelchair by the bedroom window. It was another cloudy day. She looked out the window with Millie for a minute. There was no one moving around the lake. The water sloshed and chopped, a deep and dark blue; nothing moved around it. There were no birds in the bare trees, no ducks quacking at the shore. No elderly couple walking briskly at its edge. Even the road winding round the lake was empty; stoplights blinked listlessly in the distance.

"Have fun lookin' at this," Ant laughed.

"It's pleasant enough." Millie looked up at Ant and smiled. Not a drunken, senile smile; a smug smile, even sarcastic.

"I guess."

"It's just fine. Go ahead and take the sheets out. They're a little rank, I think."

"Sure," Ant said, and picked up the plastic bag she had shoved the sheets into. She walked as stiff as Frankenstein's monster. Like a puppet.

"Oh, and dear?" Millie called, looking over her shoulder. Her eyes flashed behind the glasses. "Please close the door, could you?"

"Of course, Mrs. Aggie," Ant said, and pulled the door closed behind her.

"Mrs. Aggie? And who died and gave you manners, you red-necked hillbilly?"

Arthur was standing in his bedroom doorway, shaking atop his walker. He wore a dingy cotton robe, tattered at the heels. He sneered his quivering purple lips.

"She was so polite," Ant said.

"She was, was she? And what did you know of her? You didn't know her. What you know is only her shadow. But it lives."

"I know," Ant said. "I didn't mean that."

"What did you mean? What *could* you mean?"

"I need to take these shitty sheets to the garbage," she said, holding the bag up. It did, in fact, reek. The shit on the sheets pooled up at the bottom of the bag, and the whole thing hung down, stretched and clear, with a dark splotch of brown at the bottom. It was heavy. Ant had to twist her wrist to keep it up.

Arthur sighed, and his eyes wilted behind his glasses. "Well, go ahead then. Get rid of it."

Ant held the bag in front of her and walked stiffly out the door.

"Goodbye," Arthur said as the door closed behind her.

She dumped the sheets into the large black bin filled with a swirling pile of crusted white sheets and spots of brown shit. She stood outside the soiled linens room. Her head felt light. Her steps back towards the Aggies' apartment were thick and muffled, her ears humming dully as if she were wearing headphones, her body moving as if through water. She opened the Aggies' door.

Standing in front of the balcony window, smoking a cigarette, was a thin woman in a tight black dress and heels, curly hair pinned delicately to her head; she wore a knitted pink hat, thin and small. Her skin was white, smooth, and young. Her neck was strung with pearls. She looked like Nadine Aggie, but without the veil, and without the squatty busy-body attitude. This woman, this slender, beautiful woman, merely stood, one leg slightly bent, smoking a cigarette and watching the wind push the lake back and forth, as if this were the only thing to do in the whole world.

"Hello?" Ant said.

"Hello!" the woman turned. She smiled broadly, a full-lipped and confident smile. "My God! It's something out there, yes?" The room was dark but for a pale, overcast glow; it seemed to wrap around the woman, that grey, foggy light lazy with dust motes. Even when she moved, she seemed to be standing just on the other side of a curtain of light.

"I guess. Who the hell are you and how did you get in here?"

The woman laughed. "Ant! Darling! It's me, of course. It's Millicent Aggie!"

"No," Ant laughed. "I'm not a retard."

"I never said you were, dear. No, not at all. I think you're whip-smart, I really do. You've just got to trust me. It's me, Millie. Not so much in the flesh, really, but, you know," she laughed, "the opposite."

Ant came into the living room. Millie sat down on the couch. Her cigarette still burned.

"You should probably put that out," Ant said. She leaned against the bar and crossed her arms. "I mean, they really frown on that here. You know: all those oxygen tanks."

"Well, I don't think one is really going to kill me, do you? You know, I always thought I would die with all the parts God gave me, in my sleep, looking beautiful, at precisely the moment I was ready to go, not a minute sooner or later. Ha! I really thought that. Maybe not in those words, but that's how I felt. That one day my life would just end peacefully and I would never inconvenience anyone. Of course, when you get down to it, you can't just let go, can you? Or you get so far into your decay that you don't even notice it.

"So, I think I'll smoke anyway. I'll be doing those oxygen-carting fools a favor," she winked.

"What about Arthur?"

"Please, he used to love to smoke! It will be fine, just this one last time."

"Okay, but if we get caught, it's your ass, honey." Ant pulled a chair from the small table pushed up against the bar and sat across from the coffee table from Millie. "So, I guess you're a ghost or something?"

"Something like that. Listen, let's not worry about it. Oh! I almost forgot. Would you like some coffee or something?" Millie stood quickly. "What a terrible hostess I am! You see, its just been so long since I've been in charge of anything."

"That's fine. No thanks on the coffee," Ant said. She looked around.

Arthur's door was closed, and no sound or light came from it. Millie's bedroom door was slightly ajar, but all Ant could see through the crack was a faint light and the tall oak bedpost, an artichoke carved at the top. "This isn't really happening, is it?"

Millie laughed, sat back down. "What *really* happens, anyway?" she asked. She dragged a plate across the coffee table and dumped some ash onto it. "I've been thinking about that a lot lately. People forget I'm still in the room, and, frankly, I can't blame them; I'm not *really* there, am I? But, then again, I *am* there, because I'm there and I'm thinking about what happens."

"What happens to what?" Ant looked around nervously. She expected to wake up, or for something even stranger—like a circus—to start happening, so she could be certain it was a dream.

"Well, what happens to *us*? Like Arthur, for instance. I do apologize for him. He's been dreadful, hasn't he? But he wasn't always like that. Who would have thought, when he was a young-go-getter: that man is going to end up bitter and hateful? And me! My God, have you seen me lately? Who thinks, in their vitality and youth, doing all these big and wonderful things we think people will remember, who stops and thinks during the exciting times of their lives: someday, I will not be able to control my bowels and some poor strange woman will have to spray my backside down every morning. Who thinks of these things? Who plans this? Oh, but I'm being terribly rude. All this kind of disgusting talk, and before breakfast even! I should have offered you something."

"I'm good," Ant said.

"Wonderful. So back to what really happens," Millie pointed her dwindling cigarette at Ant. "You said, 'Is this really happening?' Well, maybe. Maybe nothing happens. Maybe anything can happen. That's what I've been thinking of lately, even though I know you can't tell. Can't tell there's anything tumbling about in this old head of mine," she leaned back and laughed, crossing a leg. "What has actually happened in my life? Ten years ago, I would have said this: I was born in Hawaii and went to school in Southern California at a time when very few women were getting an education. I taught for years in Hawaii until Pearl Harbor was bombed, and we relocated with our little Nadine to Chico where we raised her. Why Chico? That's what people always ask at this point." She leaned forward and crushed her cigarette onto the plate, blowing one last stream of smoke out the side of her mouth.

"Um, why Chico?" Ant said. She slid her sweating hands up and down her thighs. She was wearing sweatpants; she left hand-shaped smears up and down her legs. She felt like the rumpled canvas of a baggy sail, waiting for wind.

Millie laughed. "Oh, dear. I didn't mean for you to ask that. But how sweet of you. And I'm sorry if I'm boring you—you must understand, I haven't said this much in *so* long, and its hard to keep it all in, you know? So, why Chico, you ask? Well, because it wasn't established yet, just like me and Arthur. We could do so much in Chico. We taught and founded organizations and invested in businesses and we were on councils, and on and on and on. And years ago, I would have said that is what I did with my life and that it was worth it.

"What about you, Ant? What have you done with your life?"

"Well," Ant looked at the ground. She grabbed tufts of sweat-pant and pulled on them. She thought of the baby-dolls that were never in her house; she thought of all these jobless years; she thought of Billy and Stan; she thought of a shit-field and piles of junk stacked in the yard; she thought of two rooms with two televisions. She thought: nothing.

"But you'd be wrong," Millie said. "Nothing would be a false assessment, my darling. You have a sweet son and a kind husband, and as soon as we kick the bucket you can get back to them. That's fair, that's life. Clearly, I never spent enough time with Nadine, neither of us did. And now, she never spends time with us. Obviously, I can't blame her. But that's what happens. Maybe that's what I'm saying. You leave behind you a life of mixed results. Nadine will go around town and talk about how wonderful we were to Chico, what perfect parents and people we were. But she'll know better, and that's part of the legacy, too: whatever mistakes we made, secret or not, will come out one way or another through Nadine, and they'll be remembered. When she is neglectful or arrogant, or too focused on 'big accomplishments' to have a quiet night at home—and God forbid she marry or have children!—that will be us, too. Our mistakes will live on, just as our triumphs will. That's what a legacy is, that's what a life is, and who can say one thing or another, definitively, about any of it?"

Arthur's door opened. He came slowly out, sliding forward on his walker. He was dramatically thin and old next to the waking memory of his wife. "So," he said to Millie, "there you are."

She smiled. "Here I am."

His face twisted sourly, but a smile fluttered along his purple lips. His eyes softened and he forced his curved spine a little straighter. He cleared his phlegmy throat. "I suppose you'll be leaving us," he said.

"Soon," she said. "but I want to talk to Ant first."

"You won't forget me?" Arthur asked. He padded slowly closer to her.

"No." She stood, and put her thin hand over his delicate, shaking fingers. "I won't forget you, the man I love. But don't you forget that man either, Arthur."

Arthur nodded. "I'm sorry."

"But that's the thing!" she said softly. "I'm trying to get my point across to Ant, and I don't think its working. And now here you go too! Sorry? It doesn't matter. There's nothing to be sorry about. This is what *happens*. I could talk for hours and hours, Arthur, we both could, about all the things we've done and all the things we didn't do. But look at us. Look at us here," she laughed, a deep, ridiculous laugh, "in this crummy apartment on this concrete lake! What is this? This is it. All our lives, and this is it. Everything we've done, and I'd give it all, Arthur, my darling, to die a certain kind of death. With dignity. With respect. With my life intact until the very end. And this," she swept a hand across the room, across Ant, across the bedroom where her wheelchair was parked still near the window, where her slumped and empty body sat still, eyes filled with the choppy lake. "This is not what I would choose. But what choice *do* I have?" She turned to Ant. Tears broke silently down her face. "And that's the pitiful truth of it. Live all you want, my dear, but its how you die that determines how you're remembered most."

Ant stood. "Where's my purse? Maybe I should get going. I mean, if you don't need me anymore."

"No," Millie said, "you're still needed. After it all, you're still *needed*."

At that moment, Millie's bedroom door opened, and out walked a hideous and hunched figure, only a few feet tall. Its skin was the color and texture of a pickle, and it had one bulbous eye that protruded out from its forehead, blinking slowly with a red, vein-colored lid. Its arms were long and dangling, with knobby little muscles and twisted hands. It stooped over as it walked, a hump rising off its back. It wore a tattered brown shirt, cut-off denim shorts, and Converse shoes.

"Would you like some coffee?" Millie asked the creature with a smile.

"No thanks," it gargled through thick, black lips, pulling up the chair next to Ant with a grunt.

Ant stepped away. Her head still felt light. The little creature smelled like boiled eggs.

"What is the date today?" Millie turned to Ant.

"I have no idea."

"October the twenty-fifth," said the creature. It hunched over its nasty little hands, speckled blue like robin's eggs.

"Oh, God," Ant said, putting a hand to her mouth.

"You'd forgotten. And that's okay. You were so busy taking care of us, and a lot happening at home, besides. It wasn't a decision, it was circumstance. That is forgivable. I wish," she turned back to Arthur, "that I had realized that years ago, when we still had a chance with Nadine."

Arthur nodded. He looked at the ground.

Ant backed against the bar counter. She knocked over the salt shaker. She looked between Millie and the creature. Millie smiled sadly. The creature continued to look down.

"Maybe I can be more clear now," Millie said. "We have no say in when or how our lives will end. Death will be our last activity. But it should not be how we're last remembered."

Arthur wheezily sat on the arm of the couch. He leaned forward; his head resting against Millie's back; he sobbed softly.

Ant turned to the creature. It certainly wasn't anything in his appearance—never, in her most diseased imaginings would she have pictured this—or anything he said; how could she recognize a voice she'd never heard? It must have been his melancholy, his body-language—petulant and sad—the sulking, disregarded way in which the creature acted, that told her it was her son, Travis.

"I'm sorry," she whispered. Tears ran down her face.

"Ha!" Travis said, looking up. His mouth twisted and sneered. "You forgot all about me! What about Lucy? Do you cry like this when you see her? And I know she's visited you guys, so don't lie. She always talks about you. Things you're doing. You have shit in your yard! That's fuckin' hilarious!" He slapped his little knee and snorted.

"Travis!" Millie scolded, stepping toward him. Arthur remained hunched over. "Watch your mouth! You said you'd be civil. I'm sorry, Ant. I only agreed to be part of this intervention if he was polite to you. He doesn't understand how hard it is."

"Travis, I'm sorry I forgot your birthday. Yours and Lucy's. I…I never imagined…."

"What? That I existed?" A long, reptilian tongue flicked out of his mouth.

"That's not fair. I never imagined that it could still offend you. I always thought about it, but for myself. To make myself feel better."

"Well, I never got a real birthday. So, yeah, I kind of look forward to it. For *myself*."

"And I've never seen Lucy. But I'd like to. I wish I could." She sat back down, reaching haltingly towards Travis, who flinched and turned his deformed face away from her. "I wish I could see you both all the time. I've felt so bad, you don't know. I've felt like I've been a total failure and I could never tell why. But now I know. I know, and I'm sorry."

Travis stood and crossed his gangly arms over his little chest. He leaned close to Ant's face. His breath was hot. "I guess it doesn't matter. You treat Billy the same way. You might as well not even have children."

"Travis!" Millie yelled, grabbing him by the shoulder and pulling him aside. "You are being a shit. You see, Ant, this was what I was trying to prepare you for. Don't let him get to you. Just know that he's come to you. Take that much, at least."

"Ah!" said Travis. "You can have her. I don't want her anymore!" he slapped at Millie's leg and stormed over to the couch, flung himself across it and began to wail and moan, beating his fists against the leather.

"I'm sorry," Ant said, standing. The room dipped and spun. "I'm sorry." She walked around Millie and Arthur and into the kitchen. She leaned against the refrigerator and watched the living room from across the bar. Millie stood next to Arthur, rubbing his head gently; Travis was still on the couch, sobbing. That sickly grey light coming through the window throbbed, covering everything; the back of her head felt warm and tingling; everything blurred into blobs, washed over in light that wasn't light, making a dark that wasn't dark, but a white and colorless nothing, not cold, or hot, but perfectly non-existent. She blinked. The room and the people in it surged back into form. She put her hand against the counter. Travis was sitting up on the couch. They were all watching her.

"I've done the best I can," she said to Travis.

"Yes," said Millie, her hand on Arthur's shaking shoulder.

Ant turned and opened the fridge. It was practically empty, filled mostly with a stale smell. But there were a few things: a half carton of eggs, an onion, a slice of American cheese, and in the freezer, a box of hash brown patties. She pulled everything out into a pile on the counter.

"What are you doing in there?" Travis said gruffly.

Ant pulled out a cutting board and set the onion on it. She looked up at her son, who had moved from the couch and sat at the table, just on the other side of the counter from her. He looked curiously at her hands.

"I'm making breakfast," she said. "How do you like your eggs?"

He shrugged. "Scrambled is fine." His big eye seemed to shrink down a little. It no longer protruded from the side of his head.

"Do you like onions?" she asked, waving a knife in the air. "I'm sorry I don't know."

"It's fine. Yes, I like onions, but only a little," he said, and his lips thinned and turned a less sickly shade. They smacked expectantly.

She chopped the onion. The knife against the board was the only sound in the room; the sharp smell of the onion stung Ant's nose, and when she looked up to avoid it, she saw that the pale light had retreated, and there was a warm and yellow glow throughout the room. She sniffed and picked up a half-loaf of bread from the breadbox and the frozen hash browns. She looked at Travis. "Hash browns or toast?"

"Both," he said, putting his small, knobby hands on his little belly. His skin turned the color and texture of that of a little boy. "I'm pretty hungry this morning."

"You see?" Millie said, standing now next to Travis with her hand on his shoulder. Arthur was looking at them with a small smile. "It would have been nice if Nadine had done this for us, once—but, then again, we were never able to really tell her, after we'd realized it." She looked at Ant. "You will always be needed, Ant, do you understand?" Travis looked between the two women and nodded, his little feet swinging merrily over the edge of his chair.

"Yes," Ant said, cracking two eggs and dumping them into a bowl. She piled the egg shells on top of each other. "Arthur, Millie, how do you like your eggs?" she said. Ten minutes ago, Millie had asked her what she'd done with life, and her answer would have been: nothing. But now, if she were asked again, she could easily make a list: of chopped onions and buttered toast and scrambled eggs, and little as it was, it would be enough. She was making breakfast for three hungry people.

Ark

It started with the TV, an old RCA that finally broke after months on the fritz. What do you do with a broken TV? Stan's first thought was to take it out into the woods and shoot it until the screen exploded. There was a stretch of forest behind his house that belonged to the county, with smoothly rolling hills covered in pine needles and oak leaves but not many trees; he went out there carrying a .22 over one shoulder and the TV under the other arm, cord dragging in the leaves behind him. It was a cold autumn morning; a weekday; he normally would have been at work, but he was laid off.

He set the TV down in a clearing and marched off twenty steps, turned around, and lined it up in the sight. He was wearing his hunting gear, orange vest and all. It had been awhile since he'd been able to afford a license and tags. There were cobwebs on his long-billed camouflage hat. The last time he'd worn it he'd been duck hunting, squatting down in waist-deep water in a duck blind, the red sun coming up over cattails and reeds. "Pow," he said and pulled the trigger, hearing at once the silence in the county woods and the flapping of ducks out over a river; both sounds broken by the crack of a gunshot. The TV screen gave a kind of flash, exploded, bits of glass and plastic shooting out a good five feet; shotgun spray filled the red dawn sky, and three ducks stumbled, sagged, fell. He closed his eyes, wishing he would still be in that water, hunting duck, when he opened them.

But he wasn't. The question was: now what?

He couldn't very well haul a busted-out and broken TV, all its scattered pieces, all the way back to the house. Ant would be awful mad at him. Besides, what would he do with it? He went back to the house, put the rifle in the gun cabinet; went out to the shed; gave Buster Brown, his old Lab, a pat on the head; got a shovel. The other dogs, the two little mutts Ant had gotten from some kids in front of Kmart, were lying under the deck, lazily whimpering for him to come pet them, too. He went back to the TV and started digging right next to it. He dug quick. The top of the ground was hard with a slight frost, and beneath that it was just hard. With all the strength he had, he cut into the earth with the shovel, lifting up heavy loads of dirt that racked his arms and shoulders like bruising punches. He made a neat pile of red dirt—a little mound stuck with pine needles. Starting to sweat, he took off the orange vest, then the hat; he rolled up his camouflaged sleeves. All up and down his arms and back it was as though his muscles were being unfurled, as an old tarp is laid out and dusted off to get ready for the first rain. His lungs burned with the cold, early morning air—the sun was still sneaking up over the treetops—and his mouth filled with thick, stringy spit.

He made a very deep hole. It grew deeper and deeper until finally it was deep enough that a good kick sent the TV falling over into it on its side, and the whole thing disappeared. He stood next to the hole, leaning on the top of the shovel, panting; then he picked up all the pieces of glass and little bits of electronic gizmos and threw them all into the hole. He wasted no time. He quickly covered it back up, patted down the dirt, and kicked some oak leaves on top of it. Looking around, there was no way to tell that only a little while before a TV had been sitting there. He went into the backyard, which was surrounded by a tall fence and about as full as could be: an eight-by-eight aluminum shed, stacks of firewood leaning up next to it; an old aluminum boat up on sawhorses; a doghouse filled with cobwebs (Buster Brown, getting up in years, slept inside by the woodstove, and Ant let the little dogs sleep on her feet). Even on the sagging back deck, there was junk: an old refrigerator, three cat carriers; and underneath it, a yellow bathtub and three detergent buckets. On one side of the house was the goat pen, on the other, a cow pen.

Where does it all even come from? He thought. He went into the shed, which was so stuffed full of junk there was only a thin concrete aisle between two ceiling-tall stacks of boxes and bins; tools; cabinets full of screws and nails. Ant hated this shed. She hated that he would take anything anyone would give him. Back when he had a job delivering lumber for Meeks, customers remodeling their houses came to request him for their deliveries, knowing he would take whatever they had collected that no longer had a place in their vision of life. Whenever Ant's father came over he would look around the front yard—the broken down-Jeep, the Datsun up on blocks, the spare kitchen sink, the potter's wheel—and laugh, calling them "Sanford and Son." If Ant ever invited her parents over—and she didn't so much anymore—Stan would find somewhere else to be: in his shed, as if looking for something; in the goat pen, as if cleaning up the old piss-soaked straw.

Stan pulled a box down and opened it. A bike helmet and kneepads. He took it out to the woods, buried it next to the TV. He went back to the yard, got the bicycle leaning against the shed, and wheeling it through the woods, buried it next to the box. At one time, he'd thought maybe he'd ride that bike to work to save money on gas, so Ant could use the car and not have to drive him to work. Now he didn't even have a job.

He went back to the shed, lifted down a hanging bin filled with rare screws and irregular hinges. He buried it.

He dug the holes hard and fast, made them just deep enough. Dirt stuck to the hair on his forearms and mixed with the sweat that soaked straight through his clothes. He was covered with runny little patches of mud. Drops of sweat clung to the ends of his hair before falling down into the shallow holes; ran down his nose and into his salty mouth.

He buried a rake with a broken handle, a dented plastic trash can, a box of Christmas lights, three torn tarps patched with duct tape. He buried a box of yellow teacups, a plug-in Pillsbury Doughboy model, two race-cars and a box of stuffed animals he had brought home for Billy, thinking he might enjoy them. Digging into that hard, red earth—now dotted with small mounds of tilled-up dirt, conspicuous piles of leaves crusting them like toupees—Stan thought about what an odd boy Billy sometimes was. He loved him, but he was odd: he didn't like camping, hated being dirty, and spent most of his time wandering around the yard in figure eights talking to himself. Once, Ant brought him by Meeks on a Saturday when the two were out grocery shopping, and Stan pulled Billy up onto the forklift, let him pull the lever that lifted the forks. The stack of fence-boards on the lift trembled and rattled, and Billy made a sharp, low sound, like a squirrel who's found its nest toppled out of a tree. It was like he had no sense or interest in anything Stan did, like he was afraid of something. Stan didn't think the boy knew the difference between a corrugated two-by-four and a dog-eared cedar board.

He buried three of his four hammers, one ball-peen and two claw; two railroad spikes; a bundle of plastic zip ties; a roll of chicken wire. He made as few holes as possible. He arranged things in the bottom. He leaned on the shovel, panting that sharp, cold air, spitting his thick spit. His back ached, was tight like a heavy, wet towel wound into a knot; his arms were limp and numb with the constant, dull flare of muscle. It was past noon. The sun was a high and useless ball of white in the cold sky. He went inside and ate a sandwich and drank a beer. He sat for awhile in the empty house, the sweat on his back becoming a cold sheet, his arms tight and rusty. He put a log on the fire, listened to the popping of pitch, the whine of green wood, the silence held between the crackles.

He buried his beer can, his plate, and the butter knife. He buried the chair he'd sat in at the kitchen table and the spare table cloths from the cupboard— they never ate at the kitchen table anymore, anyway. It was covered with a stack of cassette tapes; Ant's filing folders with all of their receipts and bills and past due notices; Billy's drawing book; Stan's dusty tin of gun oil. They used to eat in the living room while watching TV, but now the living room was filled with two coffee tables, three rocking chairs—one sitting upside down, the rockers broken, another needing to be reupholstered; boxes of old records; a record player; two couches; three sacks of wool Ant swore she was going to make into clothes; her sewing machine; the old microwave; a dusty weight bench. So now they ate their dinner in their bedrooms. Billy had a 12-inch black and white in his room and Stan and Ant had their old RCA; most of the time, if Stan got up for seconds on dinner, he could hear through Billy's closed door that he was watching the same show as them. Except now their TV was busted and buried in the woods.

He buried his backpacking backpack, a tackle box, a fly rod missing the reel. Back in the shed, he found a box of back issues of *American Hunter*, three deer antlers he had planned to make into door handles, a window frame with no glass, a bundle of electric cords, two ropes; he buried them all in one good hole. His hands were red and blistered, crossed with little white streaks from the handle's wood grain. He set the shovel aside and his fingers curled in again as if still holding it. He opened his hands slowly to unhinge his knuckles; they popped as his fingers went out straight. He squeezed his wrists tight between his knees just to feel them again and breathed a hard, cold breath. He was wearing only his thermal underwear, soaked and saggy with sweat, sticking to his back and thighs. He looked down at himself, at the holes he made—the newest ones not as deep, not as well covered, sticking up more from the ground and covered with fewer leaves. He was filthy-dirty, spotted with mud.

Buster Brown was lying on the deck, watching him over the top of the back fence with his grey muzzle resting on his paws. He wagged his tail as if he wanted to run down and join Stan, and Stan wished he would; wished the dog's arthritic knees would let him, wished the cataracts in his eyes would clear up. Stan scratched at his beard. The sun was sinking down behind the front of the house. Anytime now Billy would be home from school, sitting alone in his room until Ant got home from work. She'd make dinner and balance their checkbook, and sigh, and say that nothing was wrong when he asked. She wouldn't look him in the eye. Billy would duck under his arms when he went to hug him. Would they ask about anything that he had buried? He looked around the yard. Would they even notice anything was gone? There was the old aluminum boat up on sawhorses, covered with a tarp. He had gotten it from his brother-in-law, planning to take it out on the High Lakes to do some fishing, but he had never been able to. No one could ever go with him, not even Buster, his old partner who now was only old; or he couldn't afford it; or he'd had to take a second job to make ends meet when work was slow. Now he didn't even have one job, and he still had no money, and the boat would have been too difficult to handle by himself.

He pulled the tarp off the boat. He was half doubled over from the soreness in his back, breathing shallow breaths, trying to lift with his throbbing legs. Pressing one hand against his lower back, he grabbed the stern with the other and heaved backwards to drag it down. The sawhorses fell over with a clatter as he clumsily pulled the boat down, dragging it by the stern through the yard. It was heavy and left two wide ruts in the ground. He stopped every ten or twelve feet, forcing his aching back up and straight, holding his breath while it throbbed and cooled. Then he'd get back to dragging. As he went by the back deck, Buster Brown rolled over and made an ecstatic noise. Sometimes the old boy would do this, pretend he was still a puppy with paws up in the air, back wiggling along the ground. But after a minute now he stopped and lay completely still, legs up and stiff, as if he'd suddenly died and rigor mortis had set in immediately; it looked like he'd be stuck like that for the rest of Stan's life.

Stan dragged the boat into the woods, over all the fresh mounds he had made. They seemed to be everywhere. He dragged the boat into a wide, clear space, set it down and began to dig. The shovel was so heavy he could barely lift it high enough to break the top of the ground; he leaned into it with all of his weight, pounding his feet down on the top of the blade to do the work he once did with his arms. The blisters on his palms seared with every rub over the handle, as if it were covered with deep and jagged grooves, the edges of which crisscrossed his hands with little white lashes. He leaned onto the shovel and made a dent in the ground. The dirt was hard and red, and no vegetables would grow in it, but trees did; he imagined there must be some sort of underground river feeding these deep, tough roots, that these tall grey trees had to draw life from somewhere. He pressed the shovel into the ground again, thought maybe he saw a bit of moisture forming up in the bottom of his hole; that he had tapped the river; that it bubbled up from some faraway and forgotten well, coming slowly at first and filled with dirt, then faster, clearer, until it came rushing out in a white-capped gush, shooting like a geyser. With new strength he flipped his boat over and climbed into it as the water shot up and out of every mound he had formed over his buried life; the water poured out with such force that the whole ground erupted in a giant wave washing towards the house; and Stan, holding on to the stern, rode his boat over the wave, and over his own roof, watching as with a thunderous whoosh it was all crushed under—the Datsun and the Jeep, the goats and the shed and Buster Brown and everything—and riding out over the yard he saw Billy struggling through the water, having just gotten off the school bus, which floated away into the distance; and Ant was there, too, home from work, and they were both splashing around and clinging to a water-pressure-treated four-by-six, bobbing in the waves; Stan reached his hand out and swept them both up at once, and set them behind him as he steered them; he steered them down the flooding street, over the tops of pine trees, across town atop a giant, screaming wave, then over the ridge, into the canyon, and away; away down into the valley and beyond, into a big green land that sucked up the water, all it could get, greedily.

But, no. Stan dug into the ground. It was dirt. Only hard, red dirt, all the way down to the center of the earth.

Short Flight

One Saturday morning, Ant and Billy stood in front of the bathroom mirror, looking back at themselves. Ant had a wide, sweet smile on her face; her glasses rested on top of her bulging cheeks. She was smoothing Billy's hair back with gel that smelled like wet dogs. Billy was expressionless and pale. They were dressed up, Billy in a grey shirt with a blue collar, and Ant in her special black muumuu with pink polka dots. Her hair was held back with silver clasps shaped like butterflies.

"To think," she was saying, "a Wright, winning something! Your father's never won anything in his life."

"Really?" Billy tried to turn and look up at her, but she held him forward by the chin. He looked up at her through the mirror.

"Well," she shrugged. "Except me. Not like they were lining up around the block or anything, but let's just say your father was lucky once in all his life, and well, here we are."

She was laughing pretty hard, but Billy was confused. He would have to remember to ask Stan about it that night, when they were all back home. Stan had gotten a one-day job helping a contractor finish the roof on a new house; Billy and Ant were going for a ride in an airplane. Billy had won the ride at the costume contest at the Rec Center the week before. Each age group had a winner, and each winner got a plane ride. Billy won for the 10-12-year-olds. He had gone dressed as shit. He had a brown felt sheet wrapped around him like a ghost, with fuzzy brown cotton balls glued all around it in log-shapes. When it was his turn on stage, he stepped forward and said, "I have a magic book and I'm going to live forever," and everyone in the audience laughed, and the judges laughed and made little marks on pieces of paper, and he won. They thought he was a dog. And, now, he was going to fly in a real airplane.

"Are you coming on the plane with me?" he asked.

"God, I hope not."

"God?"

"I mean, I'm sure it's perfectly safe."

"Safe?"

"You'll be fine," she smiled, her face sinking to his shoulder like a setting moon. She squeezed him. "I'm so proud of you."

When they were ready, they made a quick dash across the driveway to Ant's red Jeep. A drizzle fell in soft curtains from the grey sky. The pilot had called them in the morning to assure them that the flight would go on as planned. This worried Billy. Why did he need to call if it was going to go as planned? They let the Jeep warm up while the water collected on the windshield in fat little drops, smeared by the intermittent wiper into thick streaks. Billy looked out the window while Ant put on a country music station. Their mobile home looked sad in the grey weather, half hidden by trees as if it were a wounded animal trying to slink away.

"Take a good look," Travis said, "because it's the last time you're going to see it."

Billy turned around, and there was his brother, sitting in the backseat, letting a yo-yo drop from his finger. Travis was wearing a striped shirt over his pudgy belly and cut-off shorts. He had wispy blond hair sticking up unevenly from his big, round head. One eye was slightly bigger than the other.

"Cause you're gonna die!" Travis laughed.

"Travis!" Ant said. "Knock it off, or I swear…!" she looked up into the rearview mirror, adjusting it until she saw the little ghost.

"Whatever," Travis said, reaching into the folds of the seat and pulling out a dusty French fry. "How long you think this has been here?"

"Mom," Billy said.

"Oh, I'm sorry. Is this yours?" Travis held the crusty old fry out for Billy.

"No. Well, maybe, but I don't want it anymore. Mom, make him go away."

"I can't, Billy. He's your brother."

"Go away," Billy said, turning to Travis and taking a swipe at him.

"Mom!" Travis said.

"Billy!" Ant said. "Travis, this is Billy's special day, you leave him alone, okay? No more death talk. And what are you eating now?"

"M&M," Travis said.

"Gross," Ant said.

Billy crossed his arms and turned forward with a huff. Ant started the Jeep and backed slowly out of the driveway.

"Billy, get the gate, could you?"

"Make Travis do it," he said.

"Ha!" Travis said. "I can't. I'm dead. Just like you, when your precious plane crashes into the mountains."

"Travis!" Ant said.

Billy got out and slammed the door. Travis was pressing his tongue against the back window when he walked by. He got to the gate—a double gate that swung into the yard—and reached up for the latch. He pulled it slowly open. And there, blooming from the sliver of world revealed on the other side of those swinging doors, was Lucy, standing in the middle of the road. She was wearing a long blue dress with white lace at the edges, buckle shoes and knee-high socks, and was holding a basket of flowers. Her hair was long and curly, twirling in the slight wind. Rain fell around her, away from her, as if she were surrounded by a shell, and within this shell there was the blurring light of a rainbow, no one color holding long against the blue-grey street and the shimmering rainfall; but it was there, the rainbow, changing from yellow to red to purple and making the lines of Lucy's body crackle in the dreary weather with a soft, warm light.

"Hey, Billy," she said.

"Hi, Lucy." Water ran down his face, landing on his tongue and tasting like hair-gel.

"Congratulations!" she said. "I brought you flowers." She held the basket out to him, past the edge of her shell. The flowers, daisies and baby's breath and two snaking lilies, drooped in the light rain; the colors ran off the petals, pooling into greasy rivers on the pavement.

"Thanks," he grumbled. He started back to the Jeep.

"Hey," she called. "Don't let him get to you. He's just jealous."

"Okay," Billy said, but how could he tell her, tell her that it wasn't just Travis; he didn't want her there, either. He never had Ant alone, and when he did, it was the end of the day and she was tired. But today was his day, his prize, and his chance to have her all to himself. How could he tell her to leave, once and for all?

When he got back in the car, he was alone with Ant. But it was false, a temporary situation on the edge of shattering at any moment, with Travis suddenly arriving with his bitterness and spite, or Lucy with her ridiculous sweetness. They hadn't left the driveway, and already his day was ruined. He crossed his arms again and tried to bury his chin in his chest. Ant looked at him sideways, but said nothing. When she'd backed out of the driveway, she got out and closed the gate. "I guess we got a little wet after all," she said when she got back in.

"I guess," Billy said.

They drove on for awhile in silence, down Clark Road to the outskirts of town. Where the road took a wide turn to the left down into the valley, there was a hand-painted blue sign with *Paradise Airport* written in white, with a white hand pointing up to the right. Ant turned there, onto a narrow road that skirted the rising mound of a hill on one side and a sharp drop into the canyon on the other. The road was bumpy, and the groaning shocks of the bouncing Jeep sent clouds of roosting black birds scattering from the skeletal limbs of trees. At a sharp turn, the road disappeared up the other side of the hill, and all that could be seen in front of them was the curling edge of the road and beyond that, nothing but the far edge of the canyon. Between their car and those distant clumps of trees and rolling hills were no guardrails or warning signs—only a wide chasm. Heavy clouds hung like a blanket over the bottomless pit.

"Mom," Billy said, gripping his seatbelt.

"Billy, I know it's hard with Travis, but we just have to get used to the fact that even though he's gone, he's still going to drop in now and then. He's unpleasant, I know, but he's also your older brother."

"Can you slow down?" he said.

She turned to him. "Oh, my God, you're totally pale. Are you okay?"

Another car, maybe belonging to a contest winner from another age group, came speeding around the inside of the turn, scraping the side of their Jeep and clipping the tailgate. The Jeep rolled sideways over the edge of the road; Ant turned the wheel; they straightened out; they bounced and it felt like the seat was shaken loose from the car. Billy felt his head graze the roof; the only sound was groaning metal. The bottom of the canyon loomed before them, lined with boulders and cut in two by a lazy river. The flat tops of houses were scattered around the river; puffs of smoke curled up from their chimneys. The scaly grey bark of trees became enormous in their windshield and then blurred away. Billy thought they had been moving fast on the road, but now that they were rolling and bouncing down the side of the cliff, they were moving so fast he couldn't see straight or clearly. Everything that was solid became malleable and they passed through it; light melted into a darkness that rocked against them and sent them tumbling in a different direction. Ant was there, he could feel her, they said nothing to each other, not even a shout—there was no reaching out, there was no touch, but she was there, voluminous on the edge of the world. It was as though they'd been struck by lightning, and the force of the violence against them was waiting for the rippling sound of thunder to catch up, for the world's screams as it tore itself back together again. They caught a flat lip of the canyonside and were airborne. The ground yawned away from them. They were level with the tops of trees, as silent as a cloud.

A wind picked them up, gentle and weightless, a feather landing on an open palm. It lifted them to the long asphalt runway on top of the hill, where a small white plane was being wheeled out from a squat, metal hangar. Billy looked at Ant, and she looked at him; her lips were thin and she swallowed hard. Her chin and throat vibrated, her eyes enormous and wet. The Jeep tipped forward, and she smiled—a wan, sad smile. They went straight down at the ground, then flattened out just above the hangar; they sailed over the airport, and back up Clark Road, a windy highway turned into a small scratch of black in the middle of a rolling expanse of evergreen pine. They went across the town limits. The bowling alley sat huge and lonely in an empty parking lot; the trucks moving in and out of the *Paradise Post* were flat white rectangles shuttling in haphazard circles; cars rolled to a stop or moved from a standstill to an unseen order, as bugs move in human eyes, with a logic made alien by distance. Paradise stretched ahead of them, around them, away from them, and laid bare it became insignificant. Entire yards were exposed, where once they may have been hidden behind a fence or the gaudy exterior of a well-kept house: backyards were filled with broken-down cars, piles of wood, algae-green swimming pools, rusty swing-sets eroding into the ground. People say, when you look down on the world, everyone looks like ants, and Billy would agree, but it seemed to him that it was seeing their secret worlds that made everyone equal and small.

He turned to Ant, who was gripping the wheel and steering slightly as if she were controlling the car. He reached out towards her, but was held back by his seatbelt.

"This isn't how they described it at the Rec Center," she said.

Billy took hold of his seatbelt.

"Hey," Travis said, leaping up between them from the backseat. "There's our house!" he pointed.

Sure enough, there it was, their little mobile—aluminum roof shining from a circle of trees, surrounded by the fence, which seemed so tall and imposing on the ground, but so thin from here it was almost invisible. The shit-pond didn't stand out either, it merely melted into the ground and stretched away into the mountains, rolling unnoticed beneath houses and yards, just as trees that defined property lines blended against each other and marched towards the far horizon. And yet, looking harder, Billy could tell that it *was* their house from its shape, the way it sat on the lot and was surrounded by strange objects—goat pens and sheds and stacks of lumber. If he tried, he could name what each and every thing was. And Travis, kicking excitedly from the backseat, he knew it, too; he knew it was their house, and his face gleamed as it reflected in his eyes.

"Are we dead?" Billy asked Travis, but Travis sat back down and started a game of rochambo with Lucy. He was a rock, but Lucy was paper. He said she cheated, and she denied it, and they laughed and played again. He was a rock, and she was scissors. He giggled and began pumping his fist for another game. Lucy turned away, her eyes the same pregnant grey as the clouds. She smiled at Billy.

"Mom," Billy said.

"Let them play," Ant said absently, looking out the window as their house passed beneath them.

They came to a crashing rest against a thick oak tree twenty yards from the edge of the cliff. The heavy roll bar on the front of the Jeep was dented in, and one of the wheel wells was badly crushed, and the whole suspension would need repair, but otherwise the Jeep was fine. Ant would have a few bruised ribs and need stitches on her forehead. Billy broke his collarbone when he was flung against the relentless grip of his seatbelt, but he would heal. The engine rattled and came to a stop. An acorn fell on the windshield.

"Holy shit!" said the woman who had been driving the other car. She was at the edge of the road looking down at them, shaking and smoking a cigarette. "Are you alright? Man, I didn't even see you. I mean, Jesus. My heart is racing!"

Billy and Ant looked at each other, then to the empty backseat.

Clearing

Billy was out riding his bike when he heard the crashing dishes of his parents fighting. In between every crash, he could hear his mom screaming. Her yells were of sharp, hysterical blame. They rose to a certain pitch and were followed by the loud crash of dinnerware. It was getting close to dark. Billy was squeezing out the last few minutes of sunlight by taking his bike in elaborate circles around the street, never farther than five houses up or down from their own. On his ride, he noticed that theirs was the only mobile with a wooden fence surrounding it; everyone else had either a wire fence or no fence at all. The house was concealed from sight, but other sounds and smells escaped that wooden stronghold: the bleating of the goats, for example, echoed throughout the neighborhood, and their pen cast a cloud of shit-straw and piss-stink that hung over the street like a balloon. When the septic tank exploded and their yard smelled like shit, so did everyone else's; and now the screaming and crashing of his parents' fight crawled over the fence and walked up and down the street. It had no smell like their other secrets, and so came with the false lie that perhaps it was not really happening, that it would not be worth some awkward neighborly intervention; the smell of the goats brought petitions and threats, but a fight brought only a passing curiosity. Here and there, a neighbor might come to look out their front door, or a light would turn on in a previously darkened window—but after a minute the light went out, or the shades were drawn, or the person just disappeared. But for Billy the voices were unmistakable, and the walk up the driveway inescapable.

He took his bike to just the end of the driveway. He paused. A heavy *whump* and a delicate shattering sound bounced through the trees in the yard. The goats started to cry. His dad started to yell. Another dish crashed. Billy circled back away from the driveway and turned instead into their neighbor's driveway. Their yard was unfenced, so he rode straight through to a dirt trail that ran behind all of the houses. He followed it down and away, until the sound of the fight mixed with the gentle hum coming from the neighbors' houses. On his right were mobile homes; on the left, a dark pine forest maintained by the county. The trail was bumpy, lined with jagged, earthy ruts that sluiced winter rain; the loose red dirt was spotted with stringy weeds. He bounced along on rocks and the exposed, gnarled roots of trees, over thin fallen branches, around old tin cans rusted red. The trail wound away from the houses, over a hill and down another, and into a wide clearing filled with the glittering glass of broken beer bottles and the charred outline of a fire in its very center, shaped like a star. The pieces mixed together in the tiniest sparkles of brown and green and blue, the spots of clear glass turning white like diamonds, or maybe pearls. A knotty stump at the edge of the clearing had a trailing moss beard stuck with pieces of glass and two Bud cans crushed on its top. Though the brightest bits of glass still glittered, the clearing was becoming dull and grey as the setting sun reserved smaller and smaller pieces of earth to grace with light.

His tires crunched over some of the glass. He stopped and held himself up with a foot on the ground, rocking the other back and forth on the pedal. A Steller's Jay squawked in a pine branch overhead. Its black head blended into the grey dusk but its small blue body stuck out. It squawked and squawked, raspy, long and loud. Billy leaned over and picked up a smooth rock from among the shattered green of a Mickey's 40. He hucked it at the bird, but missed. The rock rose up, the darkest little dot in the sky, then disappeared into the black of the treetops with a clatter. Startled, the jay flew off with a final screech. It landed somewhere in the shadows and squawked from there.

Billy stayed until he could no longer see across the clearing, until there were only two things in the whole entire world: the deep purple of the sky and the thick black of the earth. Until anything could have been there, off in those empty woods. Until, maybe, the clearing would grow grass again, becoming a lush meadow. In among the shadows of the ground, clear pieces of glass gave a transparent white glow, mirroring the stars beginning to show in winking dots in the sky. The jagged tops of pine trees could have been the edge of a crystal clear lake. He might have been sitting on the shore of that lake, or in its reflection. He might have been looking right back at himself. He sat there until it was completely dark, waiting for something to happen.

He walked his bike home. He followed the patches of light from his neighbors' houses—here the yellow overhead light from a dining room, there the flickering blue of a TV—until he came to the tall fence of his yard. The goats bleated in their pen, a noise that meant they were hungry. The dogs were whining from somewhere. The house was quiet.

There was a string hanging from the latch on the back gate where he could reach. The latch was set on the inside of the gate—his dad could reach it easily, but Billy and his mom were both too short. He pulled the string and the rusty latch lifted and he walked his bike through. It had no kickstand so he leaned it up against a tree. The light in the kitchen window was on, but otherwise the house was dark. Izzy, one of his mom's little dogs, came sniffing at his pant leg, jumping up at his knees. He patted her head, ruffled her ears. The other two dogs whined from beneath the deck. He walked up the steps, past some old dirty buckets and a stack of bricks, onto the deck and to the sliding glass door. The door was muddy and grimy from dog noses and paws. He slid it open quietly and went inside.

There was no noise except a sliding swish from the kitchen. He went around some boxes stacked near the door, stepped over some things that had fallen into the walkway—a pillow, three picture frames fanned out, an old rotary phone. His dad was in the kitchen, sweeping up hundreds of little pieces of glass and ceramic dishes. The cupboards were all open and empty. The garbage can, normally under the sink, was in the middle of the kitchen and topped off with a dusty pile of glass. Except for a small, clean circle surrounding his dad, the floor and countertops were covered with the splintered pieces of dishware, glittering in the dull yellow kitchen light.

His dad looked up, bent over a dustpan full of glass. His beard was wiry and spotted with grey. His thin shoulders slumped in, his body bent around the broom, bent so low his spine rose up from behind his head. His eyes were softly red, like wet clay. "Careful," he said. "There's glass."

Billy nodded. "Where's Mom?"

His dad shook his head, looking down silently for what seemed a very long time. "I don't know." His hands looked enormous and heavy around the thin broom handle.

Billy put his hands in his pockets. "When is she coming back?"

His dad dabbed at a clean spot of linoleum with the edge of the broom. "I don't know," he said. He was standing at the very center of all the glass, which rolled out from him as if in waves, the remnants of the fight glittering and blue. Billy could not tell which way those waves were rolling, only that in one minute they seemed to be coming towards him, his dad riding on top, and the next they seemed to be going away, and his dad seemed very small beneath them.

Billy took a breath as deep and big as a hole. It felt like he could breathe and breathe and his lungs would only fill without ever getting full. He picked up the fallen picture frames. He listened to the sweeping in the kitchen. The glass in the top frame was cracked. It was empty. Another one had a picture of his dad, when he was much younger, standing on top of a faraway cliff with a hunting rifle in one hand and his arms raised in a V. Billy put the frames back in a stack on the table. The table was desolate in the slim yellow light from above the kitchen sink. It had once been covered with his mom's binder full of their checking account information, Billy's drawing book, old magazines—but all of those things had been swept off and lay in a pile against the wall. The lampshade was crooked. He thought about turning on another light, but there seemed to be a delicate thread holding the stillness of the room together, and that thread could very well be the cord on a lamp, the stillness edging comfortably, monotonously, into the dark like a settling tide. He turned back to the kitchen.

His dad was bent so low that his arms hung to the ground, holding the broom by the neck and the pan level with the floor, as if he might be scooping up all the glass with his bare hands. He was made of only arms and a waist. He was looking at the floor, head hanging. He took a deep breath that shuddered all across his body. It made Billy tired, made him want to go to his room, to shut himself away in the untouched quiet and dark of his bed. The light from the kitchen refracted down the hallway towards his room, it splintered around corners, lay under chairs. It hid behind the woodstove. In chunks and fragments, there was enough light to fill an entire room. He looked down. There were little bits of glass in the wiry shag carpet as far as two feet from the edge of the linoleum in the kitchen. The waves were rolling out, away from the broom, pushed by the broom; they were at Billy's feet; they were going by him, over him.

"There's more here," Billy said. He bent down and dug some out with his fingers.

"Careful," his dad said without looking up.

Billy nodded. He collected the bits into his palm. Every time he picked up one piece, he saw more. He knelt down, squatting just above the carpet. The thick pieces of brown shag were oily and smelled like dog hair. His hands became full, full of clear pieces of glass and jagged chunks of ceramic, and even the nice porcelain china they never used, that sat on the shelf and grew dusty. When he was holding too much, he went to the garbage can and dumped in all the pieces and dusted his hands clean. He went back. He listened to his dad sweeping the kitchen, then scraping the counters clean and sweeping again. Billy combed his hand across the carpet, pulling the shag this way and that, picking out the glass until no more could be found. They worked in silence. They worked in the dull light, at the edge of the crisscrossed dark. Billy dumped the last handful, and his dad stamped down all the garbage in the can with the flat of the dustpan until it held every piece of glass and broken dish; then he bagged it up and took it out.

In the morning, when Billy's mom returned with a box of new plates from Kmart, Billy and his dad were still sleeping. The goats had been fed, the dogs let in. The floor was clean. Everything was back on the table, in order; the lampshade was set straight. The cupboards were all closed.

Melvin

The first deputy on the scene put his finger right up next to Melvin's unblinking eye. What did the catatonic murderer, curled like a fetus, see? Not the deputy's finger, which could have plucked that wide-open eye from its socket with no objection from the eyelid. Not the paramedics, who carefully lifted Melvin's mother onto a gurney, covered her with a wool blanket and carted her out the door, already debating amongst themselves: had it been Melvin's hands, which left seven finger-wide bruises around her neck, or the metal edge of the end table, which left a bloody gash across her temple, that killed the old woman? That small cut became a wide question that allowed enough doubt to keep Melvin from spending the rest of his life in jail.

When they found him, he was on the floor on the other side of the room from his dead mother, half in the doorway leading into the hall. Deputy McKenzie, the first on the scene, held to the theory that Melvin fell there upon entering the room and seeing his mother, having forgotten he killed her the night before while in a drug-induced haze. But they would find no drugs in his system. A court-appointed attorney, with the aid of several respected doctors, convincingly argued Melvin had fallen there while trying to leave the room after the act, and that his shocked state was the result of his suddenly returning sanity. Coming, or going? Another small question that took on all the meaning in the world.

The police uncurled his lanky body. He was wearing nothing but a tight pair of white briefs. The dark hair all over his pale body made Melvin's skin look like moonlight shining through trees. They slipped a white t-shirt over the wild black curls of his big head and pulled jeans onto his long legs. Melvin did not move or show resistance. He let his gangly limbs bounce around between the officers until they had him dressed—all the way down to a pair of boots on his feet—and dragged him gently out the door, easing him into the patrol car; all the while Melvin staring vacantly forward, mouth slightly open and glistening. As they prepared to drive away from the scene, McKenzie flashed the lights—no siren, only one red revolution—and Melvin wailed and began to sob, tears running from his wide-open eyes.

Through a veil of tears, through the hazy darkness of that living room floor—where he had stayed for three days—through grief, through rage, did Melvin see anything of the world passing in front of him, however muddled or distorted? The police report stated that for two straight days after his arrest Melvin was silent, unresponsive, and needed to be force-fed back to health. A psychiatrist was called, deemed Melvin unfit, and sent him north to a mental health facility, where he stayed for the duration of his own short trial. He appeared not to notice anything that was happening around him.

But if he had yet to see the life now laying itself out before him, he would begin to see it during his stay up north, because by the time he returned to Paradise several years later, Melvin was around town—shopping in the grocery store, driving about in his blue Datsun hatchback, reading the newspaper during breakfast at the Spinning Wheel—as apparently normal as anyone else. Never a boisterous man or someone who seemed to need anyone's attention—he could, if he so chose, flit through the aisles of the Holiday Market and not once be seen or heard until he stood before the register, rising from behind the magazine rack as if from the foggy daydreams of the bored cashier—he was nonetheless the most conspicuous person in Paradise, noticed wherever he went.

Three things kept Melvin from seeming truly normal: the memory of the town, which knew he had killed his mother, one way or another; those light blue eyes, blinking slowly and dazed, appearing to not be looking at the paper in his hands or its words, but at their vibrations skipping towards some otherwise unseen space; and the suit. Every day, until he slowly disappeared from the town altogether, he wore an all-white, three-piece suit. A simple, quiet man, who drove around in a sputtering, smog-spewing Datsun, ate mustard-and-mayonnaise sandwiches, never seemed to wash his long hair, lived off government disability checks—and yet was never seen without that magnificent white suit.

Though at first the sight of Melvin's suit was like seeing a one-man parade—a fast-walking man in a dazzling bright suit, he had the attention of the groggy town as would the rustlings of a coming celebrity—he wore it every day, and soon its luster had been dimmed by streaks of mustard, red dust, motor oil, coffee, armpit sweat, and any number of greasy hand-shaped stains smeared across its sides and legs; so cross-hatched by dirt and oil was his shabby suit, it gave the impression of an uneven fingerprint.

Anything he did, he did in the suit. His neighbors watched once as he raked and burned piles of leaves. He moved around his yard methodically—the yard he once shared with his mother—scraping every leaf and needle away until the base of each tree was bare, circled by rake-ruts; the yard was spotless and plain, save one smoldering mound in the back corner. Melvin's suit was lined with ash and smelled like woody smoke. The neighbors noted to each other how robotically Melvin moved during his task, how rigidly he held the rake, how the level of his head never raised or lowered as he moved around the yard; did he even see what he was doing? Was he seeing anything at all? And as they reflected on this, they thought that maybe he was always just going through the motions, a silent ghost filtering into their world just enough to appear that he wasn't, in fact, elsewhere.

Perhaps Melvin began to see clearly what was before him, because shortly after this he was seen around town less and less, until finally he was gone—the car no longer in the driveway, the light in his kitchen no longer dully glowing through a heavy curtain. That he would go was no surprise; he could not stay among them in Paradise—if he had ever really returned. And everyone agreed, in principle, on where he had in fact gone. Certainly, he was in that place to which his eyes were always inwardly turned, where he had been for years, ever since he came—or went—through that hallway door, curling like a fetus on the living room carpet, eyes wide open.

Since that moment, it was agreed, he had been seeing something—an image that became a place—and it was to that place he had finally gone completely. But there were many versions in town as to what, exactly, he saw.

Did he see his mother's gasping mouth, purpling skin and bulging, angry eyes; the shock on her face as she tripped in their struggle and fell over, the shock turning slack as her head collided with the end table? Did he see the carpet rising up toward him, the threads of the shag vibrating before his ragged breath to a repeating soundtrack of his mother's cries and screams, her pleas? Was it her gurgling last breaths, choked out by a crushed windpipe; or maybe her final moan after her head split slightly open? Did he see her lying there, empty and dead, for the first time, or did he see the hallway door before him—an escape falling away? Or maybe he saw the whole final fight in reverse, winding toward the kind of demeaning comment that had kept him in her house all those years, never able to leave fully or grow up. Did she remind him that he was pathetic, or crazy, or a no-good drunk? Or did the end begin with one last moment of unrequited love, spurned by the woman for whom he had spurned all others: her sighing look at a picture of his long-gone father, the man Melvin could never know or replace? What intersection of sins would his memory take him to? Or did that murderous act really begin a long time before? If it could even be traced, would it lead through a series of lonely childhood summers spent at his mother's hip; to a picture of his mother taped to his desk in the third grade; to a hundred retreating decisions; to an aluminum boat out on Lott's Lake, looking down into the deep blue emptiness for a trolling rig shimmering in and out of the invisible? Or had he been looking forward, through his days as the town oddity in his grungy white suit, to the day he finally drove away from Paradise—to Coutelenc, down the canyon and across Whiskey Flats, up to the lookout on Sawmill Peak? What was up there in the thin clouds stretched over a pale blue sky, over a waving sea of pine trees, across the flat, brown valley? Perhaps the same thing—in every visible corner of the world and beyond—that coming sight his eyes had always numbly feared; the long hair, once brown but now mostly grey, draped across his mother's turned back.

The Storytelling Stones

Billy was brushing his teeth when Stan walked by the window leading a horse. They didn't own a horse, but there it was, taller than Stan and wide with rippling muscles, white body aglow in moonlight, being pulled gently around the edge of the shit-field bubbling in the dark. Stan had been going on nightly walks out into the neighborhood and would, most nights, find some little treasure to lug home: a milk crate, or a half-full can of motor oil. But a horse! It had to be some kind of record.

Billy quickly finished and ran outside. Stan was stomping mud from his boots on the front steps.

"Where'd it go?" Billy asked, looking around his dad. Beyond the golden porch light the yard was black and grey, lumpy with shadow.

"What?" Stan patted Billy on the top of his head. His hands were cold, but half-circles of sweat had formed beneath his arms, darkening his blue shirt.

"The horse."

"It doesn't belong to us," Stan sighed. He smelled like hay.

"But it's in our yard."

Stan moved around Billy and paused in the open doorway. "It's with the goats. I'll call around in the morning to find its owner. And then it'll be gone. So don't think about it. Don't give it a name or anything. I don't want you crying about Timmy the Horse being gone in the morning, okay? Come on, you're letting the heat out."

Billy nodded and hung his head.

"Good," Stan said, and he hung his head.

They trudged into the house as if walking through banks of snow.

Ant was sitting at the table looking over her checkbook. She didn't look up when they came in. "I don't even want to know what it is you've dragged home now," she said, holding her pen up as a warning.

"It's a horse!" Billy said, springing into her lap.

"Jesus Christ," Ant said, holding Billy with one hand and cradling her disappointed head with the other.

"Just for the night," said Stan, in the kitchen now, pouring a glass of water. "It was wandering around the street."

Ant turned, dropping Billy gently to the ground. "So now we're a halfway house for displaced horses? Stan, have you looked at our bills?"

"I'd rather not."

"Clearly."

Billy walked to his parents' room, which had a window that looked out on the goat-pen. A dim hurricane lamp hung from the high corner of the goat house—a slope-roofed monstrosity shaped more or less like a triangle, built from irregular pieces of wood that Stan had gotten free from work, back when he had a job. The fence around the yard, the cow pen, the goat pen, and all the household shelves were built from boards discarded from Meeks Lumber. There were still large piles of boards stacked around the yard, covered by dirt-smeared blue tarps, waiting for the next project.

In the lamplight, Billy could see the horse standing alone in the far corner of the pen. It was facing the fence, its massive rear towards Billy, golden tail swishing nervously. Mostly white, with big splotches of brown on its sides and legs, the horse was enormous, muscles tightened just beneath the coarse surface of its skin. It looked like it was getting ready to spring into action. Like it would step back and just jump right over the fence, kicking it down with its mighty legs as it fell in a graceful arc to freedom, releasing the goats in a shower of misshapen boards and clouds of dusty hay and straw. It didn't do this, of course; it just stood there, still and afraid, muscles tightening and tightening: for what? Billy was sure that if the horse turned around it would be tall enough that he could look it in the eye—even though he was up in the house and it was down on the ground—and that if it would let him, he could tell the horse that he had no need to be afraid. The horse, of course, would then let Billy pet him and ride him. He would never have to take the bus to school again.

Lilly and Pearl pranced around on the other side of the pen, looking first at each other and then the horse, bleating softly for its attention. They stomped their hooves against their house. Pearl dashed up to the horse's side for a quick sniff and a throaty cry before darting away. The horse took a subtle step towards the fence, getting as far into the dark corner as possible, and then stood still. Billy smacked his hand, palm up, against the window. The horse didn't turn or even notice him. Pearl bleated softly. Billy hit the window again, and the goats came rushing over, their long purple tongues sliming up the glass, stretching for Billy's open hand.

"Billy?" Ant called from the kitchen. "What are you doing in there?"

"Nothing," Billy said, looking at the horse, lowering his hand so it was level with the goat tongues on the other side. They licked wildly at the glass, their fat bodies pushing against each other for room.

The next day at school, Billy could think of nothing but the horse, that giant horse with legs taller and wider than his own body, crammed into the little pen with the goats. What did the horse think as it was led past the shit-pond? That must have been what made it so afraid. The horse was probably used to much nicer yards, yards that weren't full of shit. And it probably never had to share anything with goats before. If the horse would let him, Billy would tell him that the shit was something you get used to—that once in a while it even talked to you and told you outrageous things.

During reading time Ms. Tyler touched him on the shoulder, pulling his eyes away from the window and up towards her.

"Billy?" she smiled, whispering. "Daydreaming?"

"Yes," Billy looked down. He had been imagining that he had ridden the horse to school and had tied it to the bike rack out front. During the day, it smashed up all the other kids' bikes, and when they tried to pet it, the horse kicked them across the parking lot. When it was time for recess, Billy rode it in laps around the field while the kids in music class played trumpets.

"That's okay. I used to be a daydreamer too," Ms. Tyler said. "But let's read a little bit, okay?"

Billy nodded, opening the book in front of him but thinking of the horse and who it must belong to. Who could even own such a magnificent animal, let alone allow it to run around the neighborhood free and unwatched like that? And how silly it seemed for his dad to keep it now, locked away in that pen. He decided that when he got home, whether the horse liked it or not, he was going to ride it. He would let the horse take him wherever it wanted to go, down to Chico to the mall, up into the woods to the river—even to where the horse lived, which was probably some majestic ranch with a large corral and lots of obstacles that Billy and the horse could jump over. He wouldn't let his dad ride the horse, because his dad just wanted to keep it in the pen with the goats, stockpiling animals like he stockpiled fence boards or bags of cement.

When he got home, he went straight for the goat-pen. He opened the gate; and there were only Lilly and Pearl standing on the far side, chewing hay and blinking dumbly. The horse was gone. The only thing left of the horse was a bit of muddy ground in the corner ripped up by its hooves, and horseshoe prints here and there. The goats moved towards the open gate, and Billy closed it.

He walked slowly by the shit-field. Indents of hoofprints could be seen coming and going. If the horse was dumb, it might have thought it could get a drink from the shit. It would have wandered the edge, lowered its head, and slowly submerged into shit, its golden tail swishing up from the muck. A large bubble formed at the top of the shit, stretched out until it was thin and transparent and covered with veins, and then it popped. The smell of fresh shit came out of the bubble. Billy gagged and walked away.

Stan was wandering around the yard, looking under this or that tarp at whatever junk had been stored there, holding a deflated basketball against his hip.

"Dad?" Billy asked, "Where's the horse?"

"Horse? Right. Your mother made me take it back to where I found it. She said the owner would come looking for it." He held his arms out in resignation, a small smile forced under his bleary eyes.

"Oh."

Stan shrugged and went back to the tarp he was looking at—a long clear one over a stack of roofing paper. "It's okay. It wasn't ours. Besides, I worked on a ranch when I was fourteen and I got kicked by a horse. Almost killed me. Never sneak up on a horse, that's the lesson I learned."

"I guess."

"Catch!" Stan said, bouncing the basketball towards him. It hit the ground and rolled forward an inch before flattening out like a pancake. They stood there, looking down at the basketball disappearing into the dirt. Stan sighed. "Well, you'd better get washed up and I'd better get dinner ready."

That night, Stan went on another of his moonlit walks. Billy sat by his window for a long time. When he got tired of this he went to Ant, who was watching TV in her bedroom, sitting on the bed with a group of pillows bunched up between her back and the headboard. She patted the bed next to her and smiled when Billy walked in.

"Billy, you've been moping around all night. What happened today? Did those kids bother you at school again?"

Billy shook his head. "Mom," he said, "Where does Dad go when he walks?" He climbed up and sat in her bountiful lap.

She pulled an afghan up over both of them and rubbed his shoulder. "God knows," she laughed. Then, gently, "He's just got to clear his head, honey. He goes up and down the street and around the block. He doesn't go far."

"Is it because he doesn't have a job?" He looked at the TV. Ant was watching an old tape of *Beauty and the Beast*. The Beast was riding on top of a subway train, his leonine face a flickering grimace.

"No, that doesn't seem to bother him," she snorted. She breathed deeply and took her glasses off. Her face was blue with the soft light of the television.

Behind the TV, the lamp from the goat-pen glowed dimly.

"Are you mad at him?"

Ant turned to Billy and smiled. "Always."

"Is that why you made him get rid of the horse?"

"Ah," she said, pausing the tape. She turned Billy around so that he was facing her. "So that's what this is about? Billy—and this is exactly what I told your dad—we can't afford to keep a horse. We don't have room for a horse. I hate to say it. I'm sorry, I would love for you guys to have any and every thing you wanted. But sometimes we have to be realistic. Okay? You guys both have crazy imaginations, and that's great. But not everything can be how we imagine it, okay?"

"Okay," Billy said quietly, winding his fingers through the afghan.

"That horse probably has a good home and people who love it as much as you do."

"Okay," Billy said, but he did not feel sad for the horse.

Stan was still gone when Billy went to sleep. In the hazy entrapments of the night, Billy thought he woke to find Stan leaning over him, kissing him goodnight with his cold lips and scratchy beard. Or maybe it was a dream, because the moment was as wispy and formless as fog, and no words were spoken, and Stan disappeared again into the night and Billy fell asleep. But what a strange and simple thing to dream.

In the morning there was a note on the counter that both of his parents were gone; Ant to work and Stan to look for work, and that he was on his own for breakfast. He poured himself a bowl of cereal, ate it slowly, and went to school.

His school day was filled with restless thoughts. Ms. Tyler kept asking him questions in front of the class because he was always looking out the window; he was late from every recess and lunch. When the final bell rang, he sat like a zombie for several minutes before finally getting up to leave. The only time he was focused at all was during art: he wanted to draw a picture of the horse. He tried to conjure the image of it kicking his classmates, but it wouldn't come. Instead, the picture he drew was of his dad, standing in front of a group of spiky green trees, holding his arms out and waiting as the horse, white and golden Crayola, came galloping from the woods. The horse had a wide smile full of flat teeth, and was heading straight for Stan. Billy took the picture and hung it by a tack to the art wall at the front of the class. He stood and stared at it, and when one of his classmates—a chubby kid in a red shirt who had drawn a picture of a pumpkin—asked him, "Hey, do you like horses?" Billy said, "No." He looked at the picture for such a long time it seemed that the image of the horse and the image of his dad melted into each other: Stan absorbed the horse, and was left alone beneath the pine trees, arms open to the blank white field of paper in front of him.

Later, when Stan went out for his walk and Ant turned on her TV, Billy said goodnight and went quietly out the front door. It was a cold fall night; his breath rose before him in thin plumes. A full moon lit the street. At the end of the street were privately-owned woods that once belonged to miners—their rusted tin cans and boarded-up mine shafts could still be found there. The line of trees was thick and black, sticking up jaggedly into a light purple sky bright with stars. Up the street, moving quickly towards those woods, Billy spotted Stan's long-legged body. He followed, sticking close to the side of the road, half in the ditch that served as sidewalk and curb, slinking from mailbox to mailbox to keep from being seen. From behind Mr. Sinclair's mailbox he watched as Stan disappeared from the grey nighttime of the street, between two trees and into the dark woods. Billy ran after him.

As he, too, passed from the street, the world became shadow under the menacing and stiff branches of dark trees, their stinging needles a sightless abyss of crunching leaves and snapping branches. He went slowly, following the noise of Stan's movements.

The ground sloped down in front of him and rose up to either side. The shadowy line of forest gave way to a wide, rocky ravine between two tall hills crested with pointed trees. The moon shone a little here, and he moved quickly. He could no longer hear Stan; his own feet landed on rocks and dirt almost silently. He stayed low. His heart was racing, his mouth dry and his skin clammy. He imagined himself a soldier on a special mission, a knight sneaking into a wizard's castle, or a tracker searching for a wild beast; and yet none of it seemed as strange or magical as Stan and his secret horse.

The base of the ravine began to rise up and the hills shrank down until they met at a flat plain of land open to the light sky. There were no trees here, only ragged dirt hills and bone-white clumps of rock. Billy knelt down at the edge of the plain. On the far side of the clearing, Stan sat on a cluster of stones that looked like jagged teeth, hands on his knees, staring at the sky. Billy looked up. Huge clouds of stars swirled around the enormous moon, so clear that he could see every dark valley on its face.

When he looked back down, Stan was facing him; he lifted an arm up in a wide wave, calling him over. Billy stepped out of the shadows and walked slowly across the clearing to his dad.

"I thought someone was following me," Stan smiled. "Does your mother know you're out here?"

Billy shook his head. Stan was sitting on a big piece of stone—uneven and crushed looking. Behind it, in a wide rectangle, were more such stones in various states of crumbling. There were big, flat pieces and smaller, pointed ones, and all around them, a fine white dust. "What are you doing?" Billy asked.

Stan looked away, scratching at his wiry beard. Here, in a darkness muted to grey by the light of the moon, Billy could see glowing streaks in his dad's brown beard.

"This is where I found the horse," Stan said, rubbing his hands along his thighs. "I was just...I don't know. I thought maybe it would still be out here. I guess it went home though. Have a seat."

Billy sat next to his dad on a smaller piece of stone. It dug into his skin and he had to shift around to find a comfortable spot. He looked to where his dad had turned, toward a mild hill that disappeared at the base of a line of dark trees. They waited. Billy thought that the horse was probably sleeping by now, standing up in a barn somewhere, or else milling around with a feedbag strapped to its face. He looked away from the trees, down at the ground.

"What are all these rocks?" he said.

"I'm not sure," Stan pulled his eyes away from the trees with a sigh. "What do you think?"

They looked like pieces of granite from something that used to be one solid piece. "A bridge?"

"Could be. Or maybe an old road that no one used anymore."

Billy smiled. "Maybe it's dinosaur bones."

Stan, laughing, said, "That could be, I guess. Or the foundation for some house that burnt down awhile ago. Maybe miners lived here and they tore it up when they couldn't find any gold."

They sat in silence, watching as the moon fell down into the trees and the night grew a little darker. It became hard to see, but a little light was still held for them by the dimming stars and the stones, which glowed as if they had stored moonlight.

Stan sighed. He bent down and picked up one of the small chunks of rock, bouncing it in his hand. "Someday, when I get a ranch, we'll have horses. A whole bunch of them."

"When are we getting a ranch?"

Stan smiled down at his son. He laughed softly. "I guess I should say, *if* I get a ranch. Or *if I had* a ranch, we'd have horses." He looked down at the stone, letting it rest on his open palm.

Billy put his hand on his dad's shoulder. "I'll buy you a ranch someday, Dad," he said. Then, reaching for the stone, "Can I see?"

Stan gave him the stone, and in Billy's hand it became by turns a horseshoe, an arching bridge, a dinosaur leg, a gleaming pearl. They both looked at the stone. Billy bounced it in his hand. Between its changing shapes it was nothing but a flashing light. And when finally it ceased to change, it was a stone after all, hard and ragged.

Stan grunted approvingly. "You can't make it stay a horseshoe?"

"I guess not," Billy frowned. He tossed the stone away. It rolled in the dirt and clattered against other rocks.

"Well that's okay," Stan stood and held his hand out for Billy. "That was still a hell of a thing."

Remember Me Kindly

Roland shook a lot of hands at his wife's wake. Sweaty hands, limp hands, the hands of faceless cousins and other relatives distant or forgotten, having come out of the woodwork for what, by their demeanor, must have been some kind of jig-dancing reunion or joy-shouting celebration, some ballyhoo of a wake: one part mourning, two parts party. They met and hugged in the parking lot, hazy and boiling in the summer sun, laughing and gossiping before putting on mopey faces to condole with Roland.

He was standing out in front of St. Thomas More Church on Elliott, sweating it out in the grey wool of his only suit. He blocked the doors which led to the air-conditioned vestibule, where a small stand had been set up covered in pictures of Maxine, surrounded by sprays of flowers; little yellow petals dripped to the floor. In the shade before the doors, Roland rubbed at his fat, bald head, chewed an unlit cigar, and took to a theatric display of sobbing whenever a relative or friend came walking up. When his cousin Liz from Visalia came at him, he hugged her into the sun, squeezing her between his sweating armpits and wailing back and forth, keeping her there in the hot misery of the sun and his company as long as possible. He forced himself to cry into her shoulder, and when she said, "Roland, maybe you'd feel better out of the sun?" her own face sagging in the heat, Roland looked up at her with a dry, flat face and said: "Beat it, you phony bitch."

Aghast, she stormed away, blonde curls bouncing across her ample shoulders and flower-lined black blouse. She wore heels and a short skirt. Roland yelled after her, "Cruise for dudes at someone else's wake, floozy!"

He cackled at some wiener with a thin brown mustache, who edged around him towards the church. Roland lit his cigar, said: "Who the hell are you? Get the fuck out of my face." He took his spot in the shade again, drying his thin glasses on his shirt.

Granted, he had a considerable drunk on, but he could tell what these people all were: slime. He tried to ignore them. On the other side of the parking lot, over the heads of his paper-thin family and their shining cars, rose a green hill lined with pine trees, dotted with white canvas tents, crawling with people. Over the hill was Skyway Road, erupting with the trumpeted merriment of the Gold Nugget Days Parade. Floats, designed by children and other half-wits, rumbled down the street affixed to rusty old Fords spewing clouds of black exhaust to a raucous soundtrack of fiddles and beer-addled shouting. Grubby-faced children, smeared from head to toe in cotton candy, tugged on the floral petticoats of their grandmothers for money to buy one of the pieces of low-quality garbage housed under those white tents on the hill—turquoise pendants and knitted hats, painted wooden medallions, wind chimes, pottery; the same kind of junk you'd find at any hillbilly craft fair, only at this one the specialty was a proliferation of fool's gold. A statue of a miner, his pan filled with fool's gold; a pewter bear standing on a fingernail-sized chunk of fool's gold; necklaces and bracelets, figurines—any and everything glittering with the same false promise the whole town had been founded on. Roland barked like a dog at two stumpy old broads walking towards him, their doughy faces covered by black veils. They put gloved hands to their dismayed mouths like overripe , silver-screen damsels.

And, sure enough, when he'd caused enough of a disturbance, Margie came storming to the rescue.

She was short like Roland, with thick black hair still visible beneath streaks of silver. She had the sharp face of a whiskery rat, and brown eyes as soft as rabbit fur. Roland could sense her coming, her little hand extended out to grab him by the ear. He tried to dodge her, but she leapt up and caught him, dragging him down so his ear was level with her curled lips.

"What the fuck is your problem? You want to be an ass, do it somewhere else."

"Ah, Margie," he flailed in her grasp and they tumbled to the ground together, his heaving fat body smothering her.

"You drunken fat pig!" she yelled.

He was sure she'd broken his ear. "I'm bleeding internally," he said, picking himself up. She still clung to his ear, and as he stood, used her grip to slide upright with him.

"Good, and you can go fuck yourself too. What are you doing, barking at people, telling your cousin Morty to fuck off? Who does that? You think Max would let you do this?"

"Max is dead," he said, tugging on his freed ear. He could hear his fingers against it like a steady wind. "You've deafened me."

She kicked him in the ass. "Are you listening to yourself?"

He stared at the bent and slimy cigar in his hand. It looked like it had been through a washing machine. He tore it to shreds, the tobacco sailing away on the wind. "I can't take this, Margie," he sighed.

She stood close to him, reaching a small hand up to his shoulder. "You can't leave it either," she said quietly.

He looked down at her. He could see himself in his sister's glasses: his thick purple cheeks, beady black eyes, the circular wrinkles rippling across his face to a collection of fat folds at the back of his neck. He looked like a rotted pomegranate.

"Get yourself together," Margie said. "And Jesus! Take a mint, you reek like brandy."

"It's from last night," he said.

"Bullshit."

Roland looked out into the parking lot, at bright blasts of sunlight reflecting off windshields. Everyone was inside now except him and Margie. The parade, meanwhile, was in full swing. He could see, just before it passed behind the hill, the Calaboose: a flatbed truck with an iron-barred cage filled with drunks, their beards coated in beer suds. They would be towed gleefully up and down the street, their numbers growing throughout the afternoon. The drunks danced up and down in their little cage, and everyone laughed from the sidewalk. Then it was gone behind the hill, the laughter roaring on ahead of it. The church bell started to ring, long and hollow. Margie tugged on his arm.

"Take a minute," she said. "Come in when you're ready. But not too long." She went inside, and Roland, for the first time in weeks, was alone.

Ever since Maxine died—an aneurysm in the middle of making dinner: face down in the middle of the kitchen, her hand covered in a rosy mitt still reaching out for the oven door; her last thought had concerned the state of meatloaf—he'd had paramedics and doctors, policemen and neighbors, sisters and nieces, hovering around, feeding him, holding him, dropping off freshly baked pies, asking him questions. He'd had meetings with funeral directors, picking through memory books and urns, agonizing over farewell poetry. He'd had exhausting discussions with florists, choosing flowers, receiving flowers: every day, a new arrangement, each more extravagant than the last, arrived from a new relative or old friend, each more distantly related and remembered than the last. Margie slept over every night on the couch, and every day her husband Paul came over to drink beer and watch television silently with him. She bought him groceries and filled his cupboards. She forged his signature and paid his bills. She napped in the armchair with one eye open, following his every move. If he was on the shitter for what seemed a long time, Margie would come knocking at the door. It was as if when Maxine died, he'd reverted to a small and helpless child, and was in the process of selecting details not for a funeral, but for his own new life, a life that seemed to be filled only with various types of flowers and dreary men in black tuxedos. What a life. And Margie apparently believed that if she let him do anything alone or make any decisions he was going to slit his wrists, or else that he wouldn't do anything at all, or that maybe he'd just leave and never come back.

And maybe she was right.

He took his coat off and folded it over his arm. He walked across the parking lot. He climbed the hill amid a stream of running children and idiots with balloons. Everything smelled of grass baking in the sun—humid and thick with hovering bees and flies waiting for hot dogs to drop and sodas to spill. He bought a beer from a couple of old ladies raising money for a church youth group.

A cheer went up from all the yokels lined up street-side. Roland went over to the edge of the hill where a line of gnarly old pines maintained a ribbon of shade. He looked at the parade and sipped his beer. The applause was for a tall, burly, bearded man walking down the center of the street, dragging a scrawny and exhausted-looking donkey behind him. The man waved a meaty hand like the Queen of England. Women swooned; men diminished at his approach.

"Yay, Dan!" someone shouted, and somewhere a fiddle took up a quick, jaunty tune.

Dan was the winner of the Donkey Derby. The Derby was a race to town up the sloping ridge of the canyon, its starting point the banks of the Feather River. It simulated the founding of Paradise, wherein one lucky group of miners found a fifty-pound gold nugget in the river—bigger than the one that started San Francisco's gold rush, they said—and lugged it up the hill on the back of a donkey and started the town of Paradise, where the hopeful swarmed, staked their claims, fought and loved and killed and began lives—only to discover that the Feather River contained exactly fifty pounds of gold, and it had already been spent. Still, they remained. And still, the men of Paradise mined—some panning, some hauling dredging machines into the backwoods rivers—sucking up the silt and sediment, reforming the flow of the rivers and creating breakneck sandbars where once were swimming holes, displacing fish and frogs and newts, refusing to face the facts that all that came from that long-gone discovery was a yearly champion dragging a half-dead donkey up a hill and then down a street, to the whooping applause of all.

Roland drained his beer and threw the cup on the ground. He turned around: there was a small girl, no older than eleven or twelve, standing behind him, staring. She wore a black shirt with a yellow tiger on it and bright red tights. She had big glasses and white-blonde hair. She was holding a box of See's candy bars. She looked between him and the plastic cup on the ground.

She said, "Hey, mister, you wanna buy a chocolate bar?" Her voice sounded plugged with snot.

"No," Roland said. He swayed.

"Are you hot, buddy?" the girl said.

"I'm drunk," he said.

"I have milk chocolate and milk chocolate with almonds," she said, pushing the box towards him. "Which one you want?"

"I only eat dark chocolate." He put his arm out and leaned against the tree while he held his lowered head in the other hand.

"It's for a good cause."

"Good cause? Ha! I've heard that one before. I got shot in Korea for a good cause. Yours can't be that good."

"It's to raise money for literacy programs. Ms. Sandoval says—"

"See? No. That cause stinks. Fight communism, it sells better."

95

He staggered past her. She moved aside and watched him as he lurched onward towards the church, where Margie prowled the parking lot, one hand shading her eyes, looking for him.

"Where have you been?" Margie grabbed him by the collar and dragged him into the shade. He was sweating.

"I was helping some kid with literacy," he said.

"Literacy? What the hell are you talking about? We're waiting for you. Everyone's waiting. Father O'Flannagan has another service this afternoon."

"Why don't we wait? Do them both at the same time. Or we can swap. My dead broad for your dead broad. Don't you think that would be easier, to bury someone else's wife?" He walked past her, blinking dully. Stepping into the cool vestibule was like circling the moon; he'd crossed a border from that bright, hot world outside, into a cool, enclosed darkness, infinite and complete. His head felt light and his stomach swirled. His vision spun and he couldn't see anything; stepping forward, there began to materialize several small, dancing lights, and in their mild glow the shining outline of a picture frame, and then inside this frame was the smiling, orange face of Maxine, and in front of the picture was a guest book filled with names and sentiments. All this was on a round table, surrounded by tall sprays of yellow roses. He stood before it blinking, feeling the blast from the air-conditioning vent just above the table. One of the candles had burnt out.

Margie came behind him, put a hand on his shoulder and one on his elbow, and led him past the table and through the doors into the church. She moved sideways alongside him, like someone who is carrying something heavy through a narrow space—a large sheet of glass, or a mattress.

The priest droned on with a long prayer, and everyone lowered their heads and crossed themselves. Then the priest read scripture, and Roland looked at the ceiling—dark wooden planks that swirled up into a cone, meeting in one lightless point. When he blinked, the darkness filled with stars, purple and white and red. He couldn't stop blinking. As his eyes compulsively opened and closed, the stars became brighter and brighter, rearranging with every blink. He raced them, opening his eyes faster to catch the lingering traces of the last thing he'd seen. The priest continued wearily. Roland was sure that if he stopped blinking, his eyes would fill with tears, and he would lose it.

"In talking with the family, I learned very much about Maxine," the priest was saying. "And I would like to share with you some of their thoughts and memories of their beloved daughter, sister, wife, aunt, cousin; Maxine was many things, to many different people."

Roland's head bobbled on his shoulders. He wanted to laugh. No sound would come through his throat. What did any of these boobs know about Maxine? It wasn't like they ever had any visitors, it wasn't as if they'd had bustling social lives. No, they spent their days at home, or Roland went to the Elks Lodge for drinks while Max read the paper and watched CNN and made dinner, and that was their life—and when she died, there she was on the floor, alone for hours before anyone came in and found her. For hours. On the floor. Cold, dead, and alone. And now these strangers and liars were going to share, through a third party, no less, their memories of the great, neglected Maxine Gary. The only thought, the only memory Roland could manage: her lifeless body sprayed out across the kitchen linoleum, a black dress covered with little bunches of cherries flowing out away from her, as if she were floating in water, dipping in and out of the floor.

And yet here were more, more memories of Maxine drifting through the air and into his ear, in the reverberating monotony of the priest's voice:Maxine at Christmas with a homemade nest filled with the writhing, pink bodies of baby squirrels abandoned by their mother; Maxine's box of video-cassettes she let someone borrow one cold winter; a white owl flying low above the road in the night, suddenly appearing from the dancing shadows to smack into a windshield, lying half-dead wrapped in a towel in Maxine's hand—she didn't save the owl but had Roland bury it in the backyard with a full candlelight vigil. This was all news to Roland. He found himself slowly awakening to the church around him: the priest's voice solidified in the fog of Roland's mind and became clear; a chalky smell of powdery smoke; burning wax; a hundred hushed voices writhing behind closed lips. And where did these memories come from? Who, of all these faces wrapped in obscurity, had plucked these moments from the ether and rebuilt them, image by image, so that they formed anew in Roland's mind, so that he lived fully events he had either forgotten or never knew?

He stood, looking out over the crowd. A waving sea of heads raised towards him, each with the same blurred face, each holding the same degree of silence towards him. He stumbled down the aisle, looking into those melting faces, flickering like candles. A whooshing sound filled his ears: every aisle he walked past filled suddenly with standing people. He made it to the doorway. He was half in the vestibule. Through the tall windows looking out on the parking lot, a white light came into the room, so bright that nothing could be seen through it; the windows bloated with light. He swerved into the round table with Max's picture. She was smiling at him. He laid across the table. Candles fell over the edge. He moaned. People were yelling and crying. The sound of stampeding cattle rushed towards him. He was face to face with the picture of Maxine. His feet left the ground, and the table dipped forward; a display of flowers crashed with a whisper to the floor. The table went over and, as he rode it down, Max's picture folded under his face, and when he should have felt the hard impact with the Berber carpet, he felt a gentle landing—as if onto pillows, as if surrounded by a hundred feathery hands.

*   *   *

Time passed with Roland mostly swinging quietly on his hammock. No one came around anymore. Margie would call every day, and she'd still stop by; but when she did he let the phone ring, or pretended he was asleep. He drank beer all day; at night, he would drive over to the Elks for hard liquor and brisket sandwiches. Then, he would sleep on the porch, swinging in the hammock.

He was in the hammock now, covered with a wool blanket. Fall was coming in, and though the sun was still out, it was getting distant and cold, the mornings crisp and the evenings bone-chilling. Soon, he would have to start sleeping inside with a fire lit; or else he would sleep on the porch throughout the winter until finally he froze in the night, and weeks after the fact paramedics would come and pull the icy nylon of the hammock from his blackened skin. From there they could roll his naked, frostbitten body down a woody hill and into a cold, deep lake; and life, again, would change. One way or another, it would change.

There was a long oak branch covered with light green leaves that hung over his yard, just in his line of sight, crossing the patch of cold blue sky visible beyond the porch cover. A short, fat robin—red-chested and speckled—hopped along the branch between curly leaves. It stopped in a bare spot where there were no leaves, only the thin branch in its grasping claws, and that icy sky behind it. It bobbed up and down. It was all alone. Roland focused his eyes on it until everything around him faded to dark, and the small dot of the bird loomed in his tunneled vision. He sat up on the edge of the swinging hammock, keeping his eyes on the bird. It stopped moving, and the world seemed to stop with it; Roland held his breath. He was filled with a heavy warmth that cycloned gently through his chest, peaceful and soothing, like the jets of a hot tub. There was only quiet, the bird, and that massaging feeling deep inside him. Then the bird hopped, jumped, and flew away. Roland sat still, his heart beating rapidly. He closed his eyes.

The phone rang. It rang and rang and he stood up and went inside. It rang and rang and finally it was silent. The machine picked up: "Hi, this is Maxine. Roland and I aren't home right now, but if you leave us a message, we'll call you right back!" Beep.

It was Margie. "Jesus, Roland. You need to change that message. It's just getting…morbid. This is your sister. Call me back. Have you sent those thank-you cards? If you haven't, you'd better. I'll come over later."

He poured himself a glass of brandy, drank it down, and grabbed the keys to his truck. He drove across town to his niece's house. Ant lived in a little mobile behind a tall fence. Roland pulled his F-150 up to the front of the driveway and sat there, the engine rumbling loudly, watching the gate. Nothing moved in the yard. It had been Ant's son, Billy, whose memories the priest had shared. Roland knew nothing about Billy except that he was still a kid, and kids—even when they weren't knocking things over and making messes, or eating all of your food—made Roland nervous. He had no idea what time it was, or if anyone was home. He drove away.

He found himself at the Elks Lodge, an empty drink in his hand and his arm in a puddle on the bar.

"Jesus," he said.

"Fuckin' A, Roland, if you're going to be spillin' everywhere you've got to leave," Tucker said from the end of the bar, where he was running a towel through a glass. He was young, but missing his front teeth. He had a mullet sticking out from under a Raiders hat. He was someone's son.

"You," said Roland.

"No," said Tucker. "You!"

Roland stood. The glass tumbled to the floor. "I'm going home now."

"You should have gone home awhile ago."

"That's what you always say."

"You always make me say it," Tucker whined.

"What you don't know…" Roland said, wavering where he stood. He knocked a stool over as he turned around. "What you don't know, is that I'm your uncle. Did you know that? You wouldn't know that because you're just some kid. Or I wasn't around." He was leaning against a table in the lounge area.

"You are *too* around," Tucker yelled. "You never leave!"

"You're a terrible bartender," Roland said. "If you were in a war, some gook would eat your face off. Or I'd shoot you from behind."

Tucker threw his towel down and stormed away through the swinging kitchen doors. Roland laughed.

He was in his truck. The headlights flashed across a winding road, up into the trees; pinecones glowed like streetlamps. He breathed steadily, driving the exact speed limit with both hands tight on the wheel. It was late; there were no other cars on the road that he saw. He didn't know where he was because he was losing himself in the space between the two orbs of headlight. Inside the light, the road was a light grey ribbon, narrow and dipping, twisting through the mountains. Outside of it was a pale darkness broken by a light purple sky somewhere far off. But between the lights, just as they came together, was an elegant V shape—a dim and gloomy shade wherein road signs and yellow lane dividers could still be seen, but not clearly, as if they were only imprints or negatives of the real thing. He was thinking about that, about how when he saw a SLOW sign, he saw it first in that space between the lights where it could have been just an apparition, before it sank into the light and showed itself; how a thing could be a shadow and itself at the same time, as he awoke on his hammock to the faint blue of dawn, uncovered and freezing. The end of his nose throbbed with cold. His breath rose before him. The truck was parked at an angle in the driveway, the door still open, the cab lit up and yellow, and high-beams on, glaring into the neighbors' yard.

He got up and went inside, slept a few hours curled on the kitchen floor.

*   *   *

Roland was parked in front of the elementary school, waiting for the final bell to ring. He had parked at the high school the day before—when he had no idea how old Billy was. But he knew now because he'd called Ant to say he would pick Billy up from school and buy him ice cream. It seemed like a plausible thing for someone to do. She had been weird about it but finally agreed, and told him where and when.

The parking lot was small and right next to a playground. There was a large, spider-shaped jungle gym and a swing set, all built in a raised box filled with woodchips. Roland got out of his truck and sat on the spider. He kicked some of the woodchips around. The bell rang and streams of children began to spill out the doors. They came from everywhere around the school; from every side. They seemed to spill from the windows. Roland shuddered. A big group of them came running up to the playground, throwing their backpacks into the dirt and claiming swings and spots on the jungle gym. A few girls twirled on the balance bars. A boy leapt over his head from the top of the spider, landing in a hard cloud of dust and a spray of woodchips. The kid's shoes flashed red when he landed.

"Hey," Roland said.

"What?" said the kid, who turned around. He had puffy cheeks covered with freckles, a black eye, and a chipped front tooth.

"Dennis the Menace," Roland laughed.

The kid ran away, as they usually did when he said something. Another kid landed in the dirt near him—they seemed to be parachuting in from somewhere, some stork's nest filled only with chubby eight-year-olds with attitude—and Roland said, "Hey, kid," and the kid turned to him, a scar on his chin and dirt smeared across his shirt, and Roland said, "You know a kid named Billy?"

"I'm named Billy," the kid said, stepping towards him.

"Billy, I'm your uncle. Roland," Roland stood and opened his arms for a hug.

"You are?" said Billy.

"Yeah. I'm your grandma's brother. I'm Maxine's husband."

101

"Maxine?"

"Your dead aunt."

"My aunt is dead?" Billy became teary-eyed. "Who are you?" he cried.

"Aw, shit. Are you Billy Wright?"

"I'm Billy Marshall!"

"You little sissy. Get out of here!" Roland, arms up and growling like a bear, stomped towards him as if he were a stray dog, and the kid ran away. Roland put his hands on his hips. "What a bunch of bullshit."

"Uncle Roland?"

He turned around, and there was a little kid standing just outside the playground, pale white with short black hair, wearing a sweatshirt and jeans. He had his backpack on. He was thin, rubbing a runny nose.

"Billy?"

The kid nodded.

"Billy, I'm your uncle. Roland."

"I know. Uncle Roland."

"That's right. Good boy!" he rubbed the top of Billy's head. The boy grimaced, slinked away.

"My mom said you were picking me up." He looked around, watched a girl on the swing as she leapt off into a shower of wood that sprayed the asphalt.

Roland stood up straight. "I am."

"Okay."

They stood there looking at each other: Roland up in the playground, ankle-deep in powdery cedar chips; Billy down on the asphalt, hands in his pockets.

"Do I have to do something?" Roland asked.

Billy shrugged.

"Are you sick? Do you have a disease or something?"

"I don't think so."

"Why are you so pale? Don't you go out?"

"Not when it's sunny."

"Does your mother feed you?"

"Yes."

"You want some ice cream?"

"No."

"Something else that kids like?"

"No."

"I'll just take you home then?"

"You don't have to. I can take the bus."

"Okay," Roland said, and he nodded, and Billy nodded, and they went their separate ways. Roland sat in his truck and watched Billy line up to get on the bus. He stood there quietly, looking up at the sky or from side to side. When he got on the bus, he looked out the window. As the bus pulled out of the driveway, Roland started his truck and followed it, waiting patiently at every stop, waving cars behind him forward, and nodding to the bus driver with her "Stop" sign as she led kids across the street. When he finally saw Billy get off, he waited as the bus pulled away, a cloud of black exhaust washing over his windshield.

He rolled down his window as Billy walked past. "Hey, Billy."

Billy stopped. "Hi, Uncle Roland," he sighed.

"You want a ride the rest of the way home?"

"I live around the corner."

"That's fine. Hop in."

Billy took a deep breath, looked up and down the street, and crossed slowly. He went around the truck, eyes on the ground, and got in the passenger side. He put his seatbelt on and faced forward. Roland turned the truck around, drove ten yards, and turned down Billy's street. It was the fourth house on the right. Roland stopped in the driveway.

"Well, that was fun," he smiled.

"Thanks," Billy said, and got out, closing the door behind him.

*   *   *

"He said I smelled like booze?"

"Yeah, Roland," Ant said. "Booze! Come on, you were giving *a child* a ride home. What the fuck is wrong with you?"

Roland was standing in the kitchen, the phone pressed to his ear, stirring his Bloody Mary with a celery stalk. It was morning, and Ant had called him. "He's a kid. He doesn't even know what booze smells like."

"Well, he does now, and you're not allowed to give him rides anymore, hear me?"

"Fine. I was just trying to help you out."

"Well, help me out by not being drunk around my son. I lost two kids, Roland, and I'm not going to lose another. He's my only son." Her voice was strained.

"I want to give him a present, then." He took a drink, sucking Clamato from his lip.

"What the hell for?"

"For what he said at my wife's wake. Or what he told the priest. I want to do something nice for him."

There was silence on the phone. Then—a sigh. "Fine. You can come by tonight when he's home from school."

He hung the phone up and stood on the porch. It was early and cool, his yard shady. He looked up into the oak tree and waited for the robins. None came. All the leaves had fallen to the ground and now lay in a crunchy blanket across his uneven lawn. The branch he had watched hung, empty and bare, creaking in the wind. He drank the rest of his Bloody Mary. He sucked on a piece of ice. He went in to make another drink.

Later, he woke up on the bedroom floor. A dusty light was falling through the window. The heater—a few feet away and turned to full blast—sent a noisy wave of hot air towards him. He was sweating. He rolled onto his stomach and looked ahead of him into the closet. Clothes had fallen from their hangers and lay in a rumpled pile, spilling out into the room. A stack of shoeboxes had tumbled down, too. Groaning, Roland pulled himself up, turned the heater off, and picked up the pile of clothes. He threw them on the bed, and then he sat down on the edge of it, sweating and parched. He was wearing a pair of striped boxers and a stained white t-shirt, wool socks and loafers. It was almost four o'clock; he needed to get dressed and find a present for Billy.

"Don't know why I said that," he said with a gravelly voice. "Don't know why I said I'd get him a present. What do I have? Poor kid. Sorry, kid, I don't have anything. What do you want me to say?" He stood and rifled through the clothes on his bed, saw nothing, turned to the closet and sifted through the shirts still hanging inside. When he'd pushed them all to the side, he saw, unearthed from beneath those fallen shoeboxes, a grimy old typewriter. "Kid," he said, picking it up, blowing cobwebs from the keys. "Who says you're not lucky?"

When he got to Ant's house she was waiting for him on the porch—a warped and sad-looking porch with dark brown paint flaking off it, and large barren sections twisted and grey. A clear tarp was stapled around any open sections of what otherwise would have been an airy deck, becoming instead what looked a makeshift storage space; stacks and stacks of boxes and old furniture leaned up against the tarp. She was wearing a thin muumuu in light blue with what looked like red and yellow balloons all over it.

"Nice balloon shirt," he said with a smile. "What's that smell?" He looked around. There was a putrid, muddy stretch of yard right next to the house.

"It must be the goats. What the hell is that?"

"A typewriter."

Ant sighed, looked at her feet. She crossed her arms and, looking up at him with hard, small eyes said, "Are you drunk?"

"Not right now."

"Roland, are you alright? Mom says she hasn't talked to you; you're always gone and you never answer your phone."

"I'm hangin' out with my friends," he said, smiling his wide, toothy smile and holding the typewriter up as if it were proof. He was wearing slacks and a button-up shirt with black suspenders. His clothes were wrinkled and dirty. "You know—all the friends Max never let me hang out with. All the jerks! Ha! Yeah, and you know, living my life. Moving on, Ant, it's the most important part of mourning. Moving on." He nodded solemnly.

"Okay," she said. "Well, Billy's in his room watching TV if you still want to give him that old piece of junk. Just what we need, more junk. Gee, Roland, thanks for the junk," she muttered through the doorway. Roland followed.

Billy was, indeed, in his room watching television—some cartoon with a duck. Roland knocked on the door but Billy didn't even turn around. The kid had a small bed, neatly made, along one wall, and across the room from that a cluttered desk with a TV in the middle stood next to a closed closet. There were action figures on the floor. Billy was sitting in a fluffy armchair—strings and stuffing hanging out of the back from long cat-scratches—facing the desk, which had its own chair, a black-metal one, pushed into place.

"Hey-hey, Bill-bo," Roland said, knocking again.

Billy looked up over the edge of the chair. His eyes were wide and frightened. He calmed down when he saw Ant hovering behind Roland; Roland tried to ignore her.

"It's me, Uncle Roland. Hey, I've got you a present." He held out the typewriter.

Billy looked at Ant. He said, "Thank you."

"Do you know what this is?"

"An antique?"

Roland laughed, coming into the room. He swept some paper off the desk and put the typewriter on it next to the TV. "It's a typewriter."

"Okay," Billy said. "Thanks." He turned back to his cartoon.

"Don't you want to try the new toy Uncle Roland brought you?" Ant said. She was leaning up against the doorway now, a sour look on her face.

Billy groaned and stood up. "I guess."

"Atta boy!" Roland said, pulling the metal chair out. Billy sat down. "I think we've got it now," Roland winked at Ant, who threw her arms up and walked away.

Roland wound some paper he'd brought into the machine, lined everything up for Billy. He sat down in the armchair.

"I don't know what to write," Billy said.

"Hey, I've got an idea," Roland leaned forward, rubbing his sandpapery hands together excitedly. "Let's pretend, just for a minute, that your good old Uncle Roland died, okay? It's just a game though, so don't be sad! And then let's pretend that you're going to tell the priest something to say about him at the wake, okay? You know—like you did with your Aunt Max. Why don't you write up something real nice about Uncle Roland? Ha, ha!" He slapped his knees. Maybe he was a little drunk, after all.

"Okay," Billy said, and he turned to the typewriter and began to slowly bang away at the keys. They hammered noisily in the otherwise silent house. It took Billy a long time to find each key, but slowly the paper moved and words appeared.

Roland tried to rock back in the chair, but it didn't rock. "You have some crappy chairs in here," he said, gripping the armrests. "You know what you need? You need a nice swivel chair in here, a nice swivel chair to sit in while you type up things. Would you like that, if your Uncle Roland bought you a swivel chair?"

"I guess so," Billy said, adding a few more agonizingly slow words, and then finished, leaning back.

"Alright!" Roland stood. He pulled the paper free from the machine. "Let's see here. Let's see what you have to say about good old Uncle Roland."

The paper read:

> *Here lies Uncle Roland.*
> *He bought me a typewriter and a swivel chair.*
>
> *The end, by Billy Wright.*

Roland sniffed. He looked at Billy and forced a smile. "Well," he said, folding the paper over in half, and in half again and again. "There you have it. Hey. Good job, kiddo. Good job. Yes sir, couldn't have said it better myself. Well, I'd better get going." He shoved the paper in his pocket. "But you go ahead and enjoy that typewriter—write lots of pretty things!—and you let me know if you want that chair, okay? Alright, well, goodbye."

He turned quickly and left the room. He didn't see Ant on his way out. He stomped down the steps, through that strange smell that hung over the front of the yard, out the gate and into the street, past his truck parked in front of the driveway. He stood in the middle of the road. The sun was going down and the street had become lightless and grey. Little red bugs with long, yellow wings buzzed lazily through the air. Down the street, where it descended behind a hill, traces of sun could be seen snaking out across the horizon; but the sun itself was blocked out by overlapping lines of trees. Up the street, where the road ran beside a forest, the trees were tight together and dark. Above them a darkening sky was spotted here and there with coming stars. Crickets sang.

"And there you have it," Roland said. He took the paper out of his pocket. It was a creased and uneven mess.

The Fountain

Billy came home to an empty house. No one was there; the house was pale and grey in the dark shade, sinking towards the earth like a dour frown. Winter had come and gone and left the trees crooked and bare. Flower pots sat empty along the driveway. The sun was cold and white and didn't yet make Paradise warm or its plants blossom. Soon though, spring would flare up and dogwoods would send swirling showers of white petals through the sweet-smelling air, and a lazy shimmer of yellow and green would cover the oak. And then spring would melt away into boiling summer, and the trees would sag and their flowers wither, and everything would be dry and brittle. Billy was learning about the water cycle at school, and was beginning to see that the world moved in circles. He thought this was probably because the earth itself is round.

The goats were already bleating as he came through the gate. After many long discussions his parents had decided to get rid of them, and the cow, too. They were selling them to a tall farmer with a wobbling Adam's apple who lived in Orland, and with the money they were going to hire a septic specialist to come and fix their tank. Soon, all of Billy's friends would be gone: the goats, and the shit.

He gathered up an armful of hay, its spiny ends poking his face, and started towards the goat pen where Lilly and Pearl were bleating loudly. "I'm coming, I'm coming," he said, but as he walked by the shit, he stopped. During the winter, the heavy rains had pounded the ground into a muddy mush, and the shit had blended into the ground, making it impossible to tell where the shit ended and the earth began. Stan had put long wooden planks across the walkway to the pen, but the boards had sunk into the shitty mud and become stuck and lost. Now though, the shit was slowly retreating back to where it belonged, into a small pond, runny with toilet paper, against the side of the house—that gurgling black pipe in its very center: the shit-field was shrinking. Stan had been called back to work as winter ended and contractors were building more houses. Ant still took care of Arthur Aggie, and Billy was at school all day; there just wasn't as much shit anymore with no one home all day.

As the goats cried louder and louder—short, throaty pleas—Billy found himself transfixed before the shit. Not since the day he met the shit who thought he would live forever had he looked so long at the reeking pool. He pressed the hay against his nose to breathe in the alfalfa dust, to cover the lingering toilet smell. He had never told anyone about the talking shit, and since it never happened again, he became less sure that he had ever seen it. Or maybe the shit had just been wrong about how he'd cheated death, and *that* had been his end—the moment Billy had decided he didn't believe him. Maybe, the shit had really been shrinking ever since then, only the approach of its demise was obscured by rain.

"No way, Jose!" The shit-pond bubbled. From its edge rose the top of the familiar head. Two circles of toilet paper blinked from the rising pile. "I told you, I told you!" said the shit. "Forever!"

"No," Billy said, but he was smiling. "We're going to fix the pipe and you're going to go away."

"Aw, man!" said the shit. He was smaller now, a little shorter than Billy, and runny, less solid, shaking like Jell-O. "I thought we were pals."

Billy shrugged. "Sure, I guess."

"Great!" said the shit, squeezing his eyes shut and smiling broadly. "Hey, let me show you something!" A long arm rose from the side of the shit. It dripped bits of shit the size and shape of Hershey kisses onto the ground.

Billy stepped back, letting the hay fall. Little fingers were forming on the end of the shit's arm. The fingers were individual logs of shit, in different sizes, shapes, and colors. The hand became enormous, the fingers stretching out as long as the arm—becoming arms themselves—and little hands grew from the ends of each finger. The shit began to laugh; not his jovial, friendly laugh, but a wicked, loud laughter that shook the trees, scattering birds into the sky. Billy turned to run but the shit caught him by the hood of his sweatshirt. The shit's grip was surprisingly strong.

Billy's kicking feet left two divots in the soft ground. The shit now had

109

many arms, and each one was wrapped around Billy; he was surrounded by a squelching goo, the smell of old shit and toilet water everywhere. The world became dark as his eyes were smeared over with shit; it became silent as his ears filled with it—he could hear only the muffled laughter of the shit from very far away. He couldn't breathe, his mouth filled with shit. He felt himself being dragged down into the shit-pond. The thick feeling of the shit was replaced by a sensation of running water. It was as though he were falling through a waterfall. He fell and tumbled, rolling through the shitty water, until finally he found himself lying on his back on a dirt road; a high hot sun beat down from a blue sky, and everywhere was the sound of bees humming.

He was covered with shit. He smelled only shit. He rolled onto his side and vomited all the shit that had forced itself into his stomach. With two shitty fingers he wiped the shit from his eyelids and scraped it from his ears. He sat up.

Little cyclones of dust kicked up from the road as a hot wind passed over. In front of him the road dipped into a gravel-filled ditch spotted with weeds, and across it lay the side of a hill covered with dry grass. To his left, the rock-strewn road wound up around the hill beneath the hanging, shady arch of a cluster of trees. To his right, it circled down, disappearing miles away into a shrouded valley, dropping into a sloping canyon covered with boulders and lonely, dry trees. And beyond this, a hazy brown valley continuing into an invisible, white forever. Billy stood, and walked up the road to the shade. It was very hot—as hot as high summer—and he could feel the shit drying on him.

The sound of the humming bees grew louder. He could see a few here or there, lighting upon a dry, curled flower or just zipping by his face. The hum was so loud it became as heavy as the beating sun. As he came nearer the shade at the bend in the road, he saw the source of the oppressive sound: there was a short, circular stone fountain at the side of the hill fed by a stream of water that bubbled at its top without running over the edges. Hovering over this water, covering the fountain and floating in a thick cloud above it, were bees. They crawled across the ground and swarmed in gangs from the bristly, yellow weeds sticking up from the ditch. They were hungry and searching. Billy stopped in the center of the road and watched as the bees flicked through the air like light through the trees, unaware of him, or just not caring. The water gurgled coolly in the

110

fountain. A gentle breeze pulsed through the shade, refreshing and serene. Shit was caked to his skin and clothes. He sweated from the heat, and the sweat brought the dry shit back to life, making it reek anew.

Billy stepped forward into the shade. The bees began to fly in mad circles, buzzing angrily. A group of them flew to the side of the road and quickly tore a wilted weed to shreds. They stripped leaves from trees in their directionless violence. A shower of pine needles began to rain down into the shade around the fountain, which throbbed with their writhing mass. Billy stepped back, and the bees returned to their lazy meandering around the water.

Billy took a deep breath and turned around. On the last visible speck of road—before it turned away behind trees into the valley—he could see the slug-shaped shit, sliding slowly up the road. Listening hard, Billy could hear the jolly shit singing:

I am shit and you are shit
Shit, shit, shit,
Let's go down into the valley,
Where all the happy shit lives.
Shit, shit, shit,
Shit, shit, shit, shit, shit!

Billy turned back to the bees, now buzzing near his head. They landed on his shoulders and crawled up and down his arms, and over the tops of his shoes. They plucked bits of shit from his skin between their tiny feelers and ate it: then they fell over dead. He moved quickly into the shade, the bees screaming out as they shot through the air towards him, their stingers sticking harmlessly into his coating of shit armor. Dead bees fell from Billy left and right. He drew near to the edge of the fountain. He could hardly see through the bees. He could hear nothing but bees. Even the water was covered with a yellow layer of bees, swimming back and forth.

The fountain was half as tall as Billy and a few feet across. A thin stream of water ran down the side of the hill towards the fountain, and alongside this stream the dry, sun-beaten earth was moist and shining, covered with healthy green moss. Gripping the edge of the fountain— cool to the touch—he turned, and there was the shit, close to where Billy had first found himself. The shit paused, its eyes opening wide and a broad smile spreading across its face.

111

"Hey, buddy!" the shit said, sliding quickly towards him.

Billy took a deep breath, plugged his nose, and dunked his face through the bees and into the water. Past that layer of swimming bees, the water in the fountain became a long, deep pool, lined with glittering rocks and slimy moss. Here and there bees still swam back and forth, but mostly it was quiet and cool, and completely calm. He could see, curling beneath the rim of the stone fountain, a narrow passage filled with green, shimmering light. He pulled himself into the water completely, holding his nose with one hand and with the other dragging himself along the rocks towards the passage. Eyes stinging and lungs burning, he slipped beneath the fountain and was pulled violently through the narrow opening and into a fast-moving stream. Bouncing off rocks and scraping against rough edges of stone, Billy was pushed by a roaring rush of water, spinning him around in circles. He tried to shield his face from jagged rocks, as his nose filled with water, until he hit his face on a snarled tree root, and blood shot from his face in a thick and cloudy stream. And then, as quickly as the torrent had begun, it calmed to a steady flow. He was in a wide, flat-bottomed river, lined with smooth rocks and filled with small, silver fish.

Above him, a pleasant sun glimmered and leafy limbs threw shade over the water. He rose to the top, floating on his back, opening his face to air—sweet and cool. The sky was filled with oak leaves, and thick bunches of deer grass hung over the edge of the stream. Shit washed away from his body in chunks and slivers, until he was clean. Knobby roots curled out of the muddy riverbed into the water. Waving his arms up and down, he made a river angel—water rippling away in Billy-shaped circles. The current became slow and lazy; Billy reached out and grabbed the root of a fat oak tree and pulled himself from the water. His clothes were heavy and wet. He took off his sweatshirt and left it in a soggy pile next to the tree.

He was in a wide, flat area filled with shade. On the opposite side of the river was a dense forest of oak and pine, and a few yards off, a line of manzanita. Beyond the manzanita trees Billy could see an open place filled with light. He went towards it, ducking through the heavy, red branches, watching for ticks, as his dad had taught him. All along the ground were gnarled branches bleached white, glowing like bone. The line of trees was thicker than he imagined, and very dense, and he found himself moving through an unyielding labyrinth. Spider webs caught in his hair, and dirt clung to his sweating face. When he took two steps forward, he had to take three to the side and one backwards, because the trees were so interwoven; their trunks twisted up and around each other, their branches interlocked like puzzle pieces. But just ahead, he knew, there was some place peaceful, with shining sun and fluttering butterflies. He lay on his belly and crawled forward between the winding manzanita trunks, forcing himself through tiny cracks, shimmying on his side. He came at last to the end of the maze.

He was on the edge of a bowl-shaped depression, ringed by a thick crown of pine, sliding gently towards a grassy field filled with clover; wind sprayed the air with dandelion seed; two giant walnut trees—their leaves enormous and green—stood at the opposite end of the bowl; in their shade was a house.

The house was unfinished. It had a foundation—long, flat, and solid—and it had four tall posts at each corner, with the beginnings of a roof running between them. The far wall had been set up temporarily, with plywood. Within the structure of the house there were various posts and beams, and what looked like a room curtained off with bedsheets. On a ladder set against the roof was Stan, nailing something into the wide beam. He wore only a pair of hole-patched jeans and dusty boots; his potbelly shone in the sunlight; his hair was slicked with sweat, and he was smiling. Inside the house in an empty room, at a sink that stood atop a heavy silver pipe, Ant was washing dishes, laughing at something Stan was saying. She was wearing a summer dress, yellow and sleeveless with a splash of purple flowers at the chest. Next to the house, just beneath the walnut trees, stood a long swing set with two swings, a slide, and next to it sat a two-person rowboat. Travis was climbing to the top of the slide, his black-and-yellow-striped shirt pulled tight over his jiggling, jovial, fat belly. From the top of the slide he spotted Billy, smiled, and waved to him before sliding down into a soft patch of grass. Next to the swing set was a blue fish pond lined with mossy stone; countless frogs croaked from beneath floating purple hydrangeas. And on the other side of this, hanging from one of the low branches of the black walnut tree on a tire swing, Lucy sat—holding the rope while her long legs, white with knee-high socks, stuck through the hole in the tire. She was pushing herself in a circle so the rope wound up, then kicking off the tree and spinning wildly as the rope untangled itself. She giggled. Butterflies floated around her.

Billy sat on the edge of a dusty lip of earth and watched them. Ant came out to a flat stage of planks meant to become a porch—there were milk crates stacked up where stairs would be; she was holding a tray of cream cheese-stuffed wontons. Her long hair blew in the soft wind, as she called her family. Looking up at Billy, she cocked her head towards the house, as if to say, "Not bad, huh?" Stan winked at Billy and climbed down from the would-be roof, shoving an entire wonton into his mouth. Travis ran over, taking a wonton in each hand, and the three of them stood there on the porch laughing. Then Ant dragged a couple of lawn chairs from inside and set them in a circle. Stan sat down with a tall glass of water. Lucy came to Billy, squinting up at him through the sunlight.

"Come on Billy, it's lunchtime. We got take-out."

"Where are we?" Billy asked, sliding down onto the grass.

She took his hand. "Where do you think?"

He shrugged. Maybe it was a silly question, after all. Together, they ran across the field.

Dustin Heron lives and writes in San Francisco. He is originally from Paradise, California. His work has appeared in Transfer Magazine and Watchword. Dustin Heron is a member of the More Cowgirl Writer's Collective.